WHISTLE AND I'LL COME TO YOU

# WHISTLE AND I'LL COME TO YOU

AN IDYLL

*Agnes Sligh Turnbull*

BOSTON
HOUGHTON MIFFLIN COMPANY
1970

TO
PAUL R. REYNOLDS
WITH GRATITUDE AND AFFECTION
FOR HIS UNFAILING INTEREST AND
ENCOURAGEMENT OVER THE YEARS.

WHISTLE AND I'LL COME TO YOU

## CHAPTER ONE

IT HAD BEEN a dark, wet day, as though under the aegis of Saint Swithin, until suddenly in the late afternoon the spell was broken, the rain ceased, the June sky cleared rapidly and then burst into flaming gold and red.

"Would you look at that sunset?" Squire Weir called from the door of his stationery shop to a passer-by. "Must be in honor of the Old Girl. She's just about due." He took a large gold watch from his pocket, looked at it and nodded complacently. "Yes sir, here she comes. Right on the minute."

Sure enough. Some distance away as yet, but proceeding with a sort of slow, puffing majesty, the great black engine which drew the six o'clock train came on along Main Street toward the station. So it had run its urban course time out of mind, causing a pleasant stir in the heart of Callaway not possible of achievement by a more modest or circuitous entrance into the town. There were those now who said it was ridiculous and queer to have a railroad in the middle of Main Street and there should be a change. But like many other objections and suggestions nothing was done about this one and the Old Girl, as she was familiarly called, continued her unusual course.

There were advantages to this. The arrival of the train at six made it possible for the tradesmen and the women who clerked in the various stores along the route, as well as those housewives living there who could get a good view from their own steps or porches while supper was cooking, to watch with interest the arrival or departure of those who were transported by the Old Girl. Many fashionable young ladies of the town, who at that hour were dressed in ruffly lawn dresses and twirled parasols gracefully upon their shoulders, made it a point of strolling slowly along the platform at six o'clock as though indifferent to everything but the late afternoon sky, while the great black locomotive, filled with pride and hissing steam, drew slowly to a halt before the shabby, spreading wooden station. Then all pretense at indifference was dropped. Along with the girls a-twitter under their parasols, the matrons who had timed their late shopping to be here at this hour, a number of men set free from their shops, and a goodly sprinkling of small boys vocally avid with curiosity gathered as near the train as was seemly as though they were a welcoming or a farewell committee to the travelers.

On this particular early June afternoon with the sunset making a glory of the quiet town, it was at once seen that while a few people wanted to board the train for further stops down the valley, a surprising number of arrivals were descending the steps. These were noted by the women with frequent nudges and whispered comments. Nancy Byers had no doubt been up in the city buying a dress for her daughter's wedding. And old Ham Holden was helping Lizzie Evers down as spry as if he were fifty. And surely he couldn't be "settin' out" with Mattie not dead a year. And those two pretty girls must be the Judson cousins from Ohio. . . . So the remarks ran. But at last the arrivals were all on the platform and those intending departure were beginning to mount the steps, when like a sudden wind the coach door inside swung open and a young man with murmured apologies started to push aside those who had begun to board the train. He had all the appearance of haste even though his delay in leaving was so marked.

"What happened to you, young feller?" the conductor said petulantly as he looked at his watch. "We never let this train run late for nobody."

"Sorry," said the young man. "I must have been asleep."

He still looked slightly dazed as he stood there where he had landed so hurriedly. He was well dressed, even natty, in his boater hat, pin-striped suit and high white collar. His eyes did not sweep the crowd before him, rather they looked straight ahead and, with apparently no volition on his part, right into those of one of the girls beneath a white parasol. For a long second their eyes clung with what looked like a startled recognition of soul rather than sense, then the young man with his Gladstone bag walked hastily toward the station, was lost within it, and was seen no more.

The girls swarmed around Alice Newcombe, she whose eyes had met those of the stranger, and chattered volubly.

"Well of all the queer things, Alice, for him just to single you out to look at!" This from Betsy Hastings, a close but always outspoken friend.

"I was right in his line of vision. He couldn't very well help it," Alice replied. "Now don't be silly. I've got to get home and help with supper."

"But whoever do you suppose he *is?*"

"I haven't the slightest idea."

"Oh, I hope he will stay around this summer. An extra man is *such* a help. Well, I still say it was a queer business, his looking at you that way and him a perfect stranger!"

The parasols a-tremble with the conversation going on beneath them gradually disappeared under the shady elms of Arch Street and then separated as each girl went her own way, except for Alice and Betsy who walked together since their houses were not far apart. Alice was quiet and Betsy highly vocal.

"See you this evening," Betsy called as they turned into Pompton Avenue. "We should get out early. You never can tell what . . . well, *you know.*"

"I guess I'll be out the same time as usual," Alice replied. "See you later, Betsy."

The town of Callaway was an old one where families lived for generations, nourishing through the years deep friendships, strong as death, unshakable religious beliefs, and implacable political opinions. It had stood on the very edge of the dividing line when the War Between the States began. In the small college active at that time, there had been young men from the South and from the North. They had held a farewell dinner before they all set off to enlist in the two armies. Alice's grandfather had told her how carefree they had been that night. What an adventure they were about to have! And it would all be over in six months. They were strong in their political allegiance, of course, but stronger still in their blithe confidence. He had shown Alice his autograph album once. On one page, penned on that last gay night, one of the southern boys had written: *Don't shoot me, Dave.*

But the terrible war had gone on and on. The lighthearted boy who had written that line was killed in his first battle. And in an old stone house on the edge of town could still be seen implanted a shell. Callaway had been as close to it all as that. Now men seldom spoke of it and only an occasional tightening of the lips showed that its bitter memory was not forgotten. The town itself had remained as before, substantial, distinctive, with a quality hard to define which might have been called a dignified elegance.

Alice had reached her house, one of a row of brick ones, pressing its steps inquisitively into the sidewalk, one side joined to that of its neighbor. It had one distinguishing mark, however. Its bricks were pointed in white. She set her parasol in the hall corner, hung her rose-trimmed leghorn on the hatrack and went on back to the dining room where her mother, Mary Newcombe, plump, sweet-tempered and incurably romantic, was waiting with apparent eagerness for her daughter.

"Oh, Alice, I was so far back by the station I couldn't see well but everyone said that strange young man who almost missed getting off the train just stopped and stared at you! Did he?"

"I was right in front of the steps so he couldn't help seeing me. That's all there was to it."

"Well, that's not the way I heard it. The ones who were nearer said he just looked as though he couldn't stop. Just as if he didn't want to go on."

"Oh, Mother! Please don't be making something out of nothing."

"Well, you remember that line of Tennyson's: 'When suddenly, sweetly, strangely his eyes met hers.' Don't you remember that?"

"Oh, *Mother!*" Alice repeated, this time with more emphasis, as she went to the kitchen to consult Sally Ann who had presided there for over twenty years, about the icing of the cake. This was always left for Alice so she began on it now at once, glad of something to do.

Meanwhile the other members of the family came home. Mr. Newcombe was short, stout and genial, with an elk's tooth on his watch chain, given to jokes and old stories which his family, at least, knew almost by heart. He was president of the First National Bank and made all the customers, young and old, feel that the weathered stone building was a friendly place as long as Bill Newcombe with his wide smile and jolly laugh was looking after it. There was a more pertinent reason why they felt their bank president stood for security: Newcombe's eyes could look cold and shrewd upon occasion and there was a saying abroad that he had a sixth sense when it came to buying or selling negotiable assets.

Tom, his son, who came in after him now, was more like his mother except for his height. He had thoughtful looking dark eyes and a smile which all the girls said was too sweet to be wasted on a boy.

Mrs. Newcombe greeted her menfolk warmly as usual, then a little later when she felt they had had time to perform their hasty ablutions above, she tapped the wooden Chinese gongs which hung on cords from their rack in the dining room, and Sally Ann appeared in the kitchen doorway to announce somewhat unnecessarily that dinner was served. Alice followed the men down the front stairs and the family settled themselves to the evening meal. There was a completely unintelligible though never omitted grace (Mr. Newcombe evidently feeling that he was addressing the Almighty and it made no difference whether others understood it or not), then as the carving started, so did conversation.

"I hear you held the strange young man spellbound," Tom began, looking mischievously at his sister.

"What's that? What's that?" inquired Newcombe, with the carving knife poised.

"Now, Tom, you mustn't tease Alice. She couldn't help it. The young man was asleep he told the conductor and nearly missed getting off the train. He seemed flustered when he finally got to the last step and saw some of the girls right in front of him and Alice was nearest. That was all, wasn't it, dear?"

"It certainly was. And I'll thank you, Tom, not to go round spreading silly rumors."

"Now, what have *I* done?" Tom asked pathetically. "I only repeated what the other fellows told me. After all," he added ingratiatingly, "even if you are my sister, you aren't hard to look at."

"Now, I consider that a nice remark for a brother to make!" Mrs. Newcombe's round face radiated satisfaction. "And we'll say no more about the . . . the incident. But," she added so hastily that Alice laughed, "did any of the boys see where the young man went, Tom?"

"Not a trace. He seemed to vanish into thin air."

"And now," said Mr. Newcombe crisply, laying down his carving implements, "I'm ready to hear what you're all talking about. Suppose, Alice, you tell it to me straight."

Alice gave the facts briefly and her father looked crestfallen.

"Huh! Is that all? From the bits I heard I thought there was some kind of romantic mystery abroad. Well, I must say I'm just as well satisfied."

General conversation flowed back and forth as usual with now and then a veiled reference to the stranger in town until Sally Ann's layer cake had all been consumed. Then Alice said briskly, "You might as well get out the carpet, Tom, Betsy said she would be down early."

"Oh, she did, did she?" Tom said as he excused himself and left the table. "I wonder why!" His voice had a faint edge.

"He doesn't show it much," Mrs. Newcombe said in a low tone, "but I think Tom is fond of Betsy."

There were in Callaway in the summer evenings three forms of diversion or entertainment. The first and simplest was the gathering of young people on the steps of the more popular houses where a strip of carpet — rag, ingrain or Brussels — had been spread and well covered with cushions. Here the girls sat prettily, the boys stood or lounged near, while gossip and young laughter went on until dusk when the singing usually began. Often groups within hearing of each other would vie to see whose voices would carry farthest; but oftener still there was a friendly harmonizing so that waves of music rolled along from street to street.

While the gossip, laughter and singing would seem to the uninitiate as though nothing but young gaiety went on at these parties on the steps, there were, withal, many a clasping of hand with hand beneath the soft folds of a dress and many a tender proximity of head to head as the dusk blurred the outline of the faces.

The second favorite pastime was a trolley ride. Of course many families had their own horses and carriages, for the day of the auto was still not quite breaking on the horizon, so meanwhile, swinging along with what in summer seemed delirious speed, were the trolleys. In the warm evenings the long hospitable seats invited occupants and the wide open sides allowed the rushing air and the flying scenes to keep pace with the occasional clanging of the bell as Mr. Emory, the motorman, inspired by his own mastery of time and space, stood erect at the front of the car and guided it on its way, not only through the town but around the creek and even as far as Henderson's Falls, three miles from Callaway, where there were real farm fields of hay and clover, the

sweet odors of which brought romance to the trolley riders.
Mr. Emory, already assured of enough fares for the longer
ride, always went slowly past Henderson's Mill and around
the fields, for, while to look at him you would never guess it,
he had once been young and romantic himself.

There was one other evening diversion, perhaps the most
intimate of all. This was boating, or more likely canoeing,
on the gentle Canodoquinnett Creek which flowed past the
southern end of the town. Here often a pair of young people
came when they wished to be alone. Of course others had
the same idea and a number of canoes could always be
spotted here and there with soft little bursts of song emanat-
ing from them, often boating songs which another genera-
tion had sent over the quiet waters and then passed on to
their children.

> Oh, who will raise my green umbrella
> When I am far away?

Or perhaps:

> Now Moses you watch it! Now Moses you'll catch it!
> Now Moses do you hear what I say?

with the haunting, recurring refrain:

> 'Tis sweet to be remembered. . . .

But those in the canoes did not mind the distant cadences.
They only emphasized pleasantly their own removal,

whether as lovers or friends, from a world in which just then they wished no part.

Tonight, as Alice had intimated to Tom, they would entertain on the steps and she hurried, too, to prepare the scene. Their strip of carpet was red and partook of Brussels elegance, as it had been left over from the new covering for the back parlor. She brought the cushions from the bottom of the hall closet, arranged them with a care that she hoped would look casual, then went upstairs to dress.

"I think I'd wear the flowered lawn, Alice," her mother called from the doorway, "not that it really matters but then you never know . . ." Her voice trailed off as it always did when anything bordering upon romance touched it.

Alice merely waved over the stairwell and went on. Though outwardly disclaiming any feeling whatever over the odd occurrence at the train platform that afternoon, she had been more deeply moved by it than by anything that had previously happened to her. When the eyes of the stranger suddenly not only met her own but held them to his she felt as though some sort of shock had penetrated her being. She had then felt amazed, troubled, anxious. She still did. She longed to see him again and scorned herself for the desire. She hoped the strange feelings would leave her, then grieved to think they might. It was beyond all bounds of possibility that he would find his way to their steps tonight, yet *someone* might have learned his whereabouts and told him of the step parties. Betsy Hastings would most certainly put her brother on the chase. Ah — Alice breathed suddenly and sank down upon the side of the bed.

George Hastings! The thought of him brought her up short with present reality, for during the last six months he had been pressing upon her the attention which in Callaway, as in most towns, led up to a proposal of marriage. And she herself with a little flutter of the heart had been in the main ready for such a climax. Until this afternoon. Then because of the sudden meeting of eyes with eyes, or could it have been spirit with spirit, she was uncertain and confused. She had always known George since he pulled her sled up the hill for her. He was big and blond and jolly and there had never seemed an earthly reason why she shouldn't marry him. Until now.

Alice brushed her hair vigorously, arranged her pompadour three times over and told herself she was a fool. She slipped the flowered lawn over her shoulders, finally found herself ready and descended the stairs.

It was none too soon for the arrival of the guests. Betsy, dark and animated, was already there talking to Tom. He turned to his sister. "Betsy says George was talking to the station agent and he said the strange young fellah went past him like a shot and hurried out the back door and along Windsor Road."

"Windsor Road?" Alice echoed in surprise. "Why there's hardly a house there except the Adair place."

"That's just it," Betsy said. "I believe that's where he was going. They haven't a relative in the whole country they often say, but they're great for keeping up with all their old friends and their children and grandchildren and so on. Oh, Alice, George said to tell you he won't be here tonight. The foremen at the factory are called to a meeting. George was very put out but he couldn't help it."

"Of course not," Alice said. "That's all right. We'll miss his tenor, though, if we sing."

The steps gradually filled and the laughter and jokes began as usual with many inventive suppositions about the newcomer thrown in. If he really *was* a stranger how had he known to go out Windsor Road?

"He could have had directions in a letter," someone suggested.

"Well now," Matt Barnes began with a fine mixture of mystery and complacence, "I've been waiting to spring a small bit of news on you. Mr. Giles at the station seemed willing enough to talk to me. I help him with the baggage sometimes. Well, he said he had a good view of the young fellah's bag and it had initials on it."

"Oh, Matt, *what?*" came the chorus.

"They were R. R. A. Now what I think is that the *A* stands for Adair and he's a forty-second cousin the old ladies didn't know they had until recently and now he's come as fast as he can to introduce himself and . . ."

"And get their money!" Betsy finished impulsively.

"Oh, don't even think such a horrid thing," Alice said. "Let's drop the whole matter until we really know something definite. If we go on surmising, who knows where we'll end up. How about some cake?"

There was quick acclaim. While refreshments were not considered obligatory at the steps parties they were decidedly well received when occasionally provided. In a short time now, the luscious work of Sally Ann's hands, accompanied by the lemonade the boys made with much laughter in the kitchen, were partaken of, and the evening ended earlier than usual, with a few songs and the somewhat self-conscious pairing off of the young people before they separated for the neighboring streets. Betsy stayed behind, for Tom would see her home.

"And let's leave it," she said earnestly to Alice, "that if either of us hears anything tomorrow we'll each let the other know. All right?"

"Of course," Alice said, trying to laugh.

But lying quietly in her fourposter bed that night she did not feel like laughing. The strange feelings of the late afternoon had not only returned but had, added to them, the ugly suggestion of Betsy's remark. With no volition on her part her mind began to go over the life of Miss Kitty and Miss Jenny Adair as she had known it and heard it from her parents.

The Adair residence was by far the handsomest one in town. A large and beautiful stone edifice rose from the center of a green and flowered lawn which must have comprised a city block. Old Colonel Adair, who had made his money in the carpet mill at the opposite edge of the town, had long ago left a fortune to his motherless daughters. There was the steady income from the mill, which under good management had gone on developing year after year and upon which the sisters lived in great comfort. There had also certainly been a large amount of money which the town had never ceased to puzzle over. For no one had ever learned how much this was nor how it had been placed, even though many bankers, bond salesmen and general investors had made oblique efforts. To all and sundry, Miss Kitty and Miss Jenny had merely answered complacently that their finances were quite safe and would say nothing more.

Mr. Newcombe, as president of the bank and an old and, he felt, trusted friend, was the most concerned.

"They're so innocent, so naive," he kept telling his wife, "there's simply no knowing what sort of crazy wildcat scheme they may have taken up with. I feel responsible in a way, but you can't get a word out of them. They keep a good checking account, but they don't have any savings or a lock-box with us or in any other bank in the Valley, for I've made it my business to find out."

"Don't worry," Mrs. Newcombe always answered. "They have plenty from the mill to live on and they are so kind and generous and dear, we shouldn't question their affairs."

Alice had heard the substance of this conversation many times without paying too much heed to it, but now the possibility of a large, hidden fortune which one day must be left as an inheritance, coupled with Betsy's groundless insinuation about the strange young man, brought a peculiar pang to her heart. He didn't look like a fortune hunter. During that strange brief glance his eyes had seemed honest and straightforward . . . It was a long time before she went to sleep. Then it was to the midst of a dream that the owner of the initials on the bag was really staying at the home of Miss Kitty and Miss Jenny Adair.

The dream was true, as all those interested were to discover the next day through a chance remark of Molly Hart whom the Adair ladies had (in the town's parlance) raised from a very young girl. Not being blessed with either beauty or form to attract the opposite sex, but strong, capable and devoted to her benefactors, Molly had continued to live on contentedly in the great house, as half domestic, half companion. It was her statement to Mr. Weir, the stationer, that caused the lines of gossip to vibrate.

"It's a comfort," she said dreamily, "not to lock up at night as if you were in a jail. With a young man in the house you don't have to be so careful."

Squire Weir peered sharply through his steel-rimmed glasses. "Oh, you have a young man in the house, do you?"

Molly turned red and shut up like a clam. She took the package of blue notepaper, paid the bill, and left precipitately. But the secret was out, at least enough to build upon substantially.

It was less than a week later that the blue notes were left by the early post at the homes of all the town's elite. Mrs. Newcombe read hers quickly, and rushed up to show it to Alice, who had not finished dressing. Their heads bent together over it.

The Misses Adair cordially invite Mr. and Mrs. Newcombe and family to a soiree on Friday evening the tenth of June from seven until ten o'clock. The favor of a reply is requested.

"Now *what* do you suppose prompted this? They haven't entertained in a long time. Do you suppose it has anything to do with the young man?" Mrs. Newcombe said. "And Alice, if I hurry I'm sure I can have your new white organdy finished. This really calls for something special. I'm glad my surah silk is practically new. Well, it is exciting, isn't it?"

Alice stood by her bedroom door. She had been brushing her hair when her mother had hurried up with the blue note. Now, she paused, considering, her hair hanging over her shoulders, while her mother for the thousandth time wondered how she and Bill had produced anything as lovely as their daughter. For the blond of her hair had definite gold in it, her lashes were long and dark, shadowing eyes that were more gray than blue, her cheeks were not round and rosy like Betsy's but more gently molded and colored, her smile was slow but of an unusual sweetness when it did come. Her laughter was pure music.

Sometimes in the still hours of the night, not being able to keep her thoughts to herself any longer, Mary would wake her husband.

"About Alice, Bill."

"Wha . . . what about her?"

"Don't you think she's getting prettier all the time?"

"Well, yes. I think she is."

"I've been wondering. She's so gentle usually, but she has a very strong will too. Maybe that's a combination of the two of us."

"Maybe. Well, we did a good job between us."

"But Bill. Do you think George Hastings is good enough for her?"

"No man's good enough for your daughter. So let's leave it at that and get back to sleep, for Pete's sake."

With a heightened color, now, Alice was starting to discuss the matter in hand. Yes, she thought the soiree might quite likely have something to do with the young man visitor, if he really *was* there. Yes, she would like to have the white organdy to wear and would help hem the ruffles. And yes, she agreed it would be exciting to go to a big party like this, for there hadn't been one for so long. It was sweet of Miss Jenny and Miss Kitty to invite the young people too. Of course if this was in honor of the guest they would naturally . . . It was always lovely to go to their house for any reason and now the rose garden would be in bloom and probably they could be outside much of the time.

"Do you suppose," she added, "that Grandfather will be invited?"

"Of course," her mother said. "When did they ever leave him out?"

"I wonder," Alice said thoughtfully as she moved back into her bedroom, "if there was ever a romance between him and Miss Jenny?"

"Well, you'll never find it out from either of them if there was," her mother returned, as she started back to the sewing room.

"I may run over to visit with Grandfather a few minutes," Alice called after her. "If I hurry I may catch him at breakfast and have it with him."

When she was ready she started hurriedly down Poplar Avenue with a sharp eye to spot and intercept Betsy or any of the other girls if they should appear, blue notes in hand, and finally reached by means of a narrow macadam and a still narrower path, the white frame house on a back street on the edge of a quiet bit of woodland where David Means lived. The wide porch and upper gables had intricate "ginger-bread" trimmings which her grandfather said lightened his spirits after the unrelieved brick and stone of most of the other town dwellings. Alice could see the old gentleman now on the porch, gray hair neatly brushed, his gray moustache neatly trimmed, sitting in the large chair with the writing arm where he spent most of his days. She ran the last few steps and arrived breathless.

"Oh, Grandpa," she burst out, "I don't know what I'd do if I hadn't you to talk to. I'm so mixed up."

He put a kiss on her cheek. "Well, I'll admit things seem to have been happening, but you have a pretty clear head. Why don't you begin with the station platform episode?"

"Oh, you *know* about that!"

"Why wouldn't I know in this town? As a matter of fact I've had three versions already. (a) The young man was half asleep and didn't know what or whom he was looking at. (b) He stared at you with stark admiration, for which I don't blame him. (c) He looked at you as if it was love at first sight. Now, let's have *your* story."

Alice sat on a wicker hassock close beside him, and clasped her arms about her knees.

"That's the trouble. I simply don't know, but I have felt a bit strange ever since. Just like a nice calm little bit of water that has a stone dropped in it."

"So you were conscious of some ripples?"

"Yes, and it bothers me. Such a little matter of two people looking at each other shouldn't cause any disturbance of mind, now, should it?"

"Well as I recall," her grandfather said calmly, "Dante was just casually walking down the street when he saw Beatrice, and after that there was disturbance a-plenty."

"Oh, *you!*" Alice laughed. "You're worse than Mother. She was quoting Tennyson, as usual. I just wanted to talk sense with you . . ."

"I suppose from the facts already known your mother is starting to make your wedding gown," he chuckled.

"Not quite that, but she is trying to finish my white organdy for the soiree. You're invited?" Alice asked eagerly.

"Oh, yes."

"And you're going?"

"I suppose so. I'm curious."

"Well, I *want* you to be there so we can talk it over afterwards. Why do the threads of life get so ridiculously tangled up?" she added with a sigh.

"I would take that to mean George Hastings," her grandfather said gently.

"I suppose he's one of the threads. Have you had breakfast? Good. May I have it out here with you? It's such a comfort to talk to you, for at home I have disclaimed the slightest feeling about the . . . the incident at the station. But you don't think I'm silly to have thought about it."

"Not at all," her grandfather said, "but if I were you I wouldn't dwell too much upon it. Just drink the cup of life as it comes and don't stir it up from the bottom. What baffles me is just what connection this young man has with the Adair girls. That's why I'm going to the soiree to find out."

"Grandpa, couldn't we pick you up that night? Wouldn't you go with us?" her voice was pleading. "We'll use the carriage."

"Oh, I'll probably just drive Prince out, but thanks anyway. Here comes breakfast."

On the way home, the girl thought again of the strange situation in her immediate family. The fact was that her own father and her mother's father did not like each other and there was therefore no contact between them. Just what had actually caused such a sharp and lasting breach she did not know, but both men were strong-willed and determined. Her mother would not discuss it, though she visited her father often. Tom went too, and Alice found the big frame house on the edge of the woods a constant haven, for she and her grandfather were deeply congenial. She had once made a last effort to solve the mystery. She knew that he went to Sunday dinner occasionally at the Miss Adairs' and sometimes of an evening also, so she approached Miss Jenny who the town believed had once been his sweetheart and asked the question: Just what was the reason for the enmity between David Means, her grandfather, and William Newcombe, her father?

Miss Jenny had flushed to the roots of her hair even at her age, for she at once recalled the time she had asked David the same question. He had then pulled one ear meditatively and said that William's eyes were set too close together. Then he had added as though in a full burst of confession, "He's too *hearty* for me, Jenny. He wears me out." And that was all. So Miss Jenny had answered Alice quite truthfully, "I don't know, my dear. I honestly don't know."

As the time for the soiree approached, the town's first families were caught up in a vortex of suspense. Miss Hilda Carns, the dressmaker, sewed far into the night, and other non-professionals bent over their sewing machines with eager haste to complete the filmy ruffles and flounces which would grace the young girls' costumes on this occasion. One thing all realized, though they did not voice it. That was the fact that they were still all oppressed by the burden of conjecture. For in spite of what seemed unmistakable hints and the approaching soiree itself, the strange young man had never been seen since the day he had dismounted from the train. Could there be a mistake after all?

The day of the soiree was one of June's finest. Even as the evening neared seven there was a pleasant warmth in the air and circling around the sky as though the sunset was determined not to be partial to the west, were long banking clouds of deep gold and rose. The Newcombes' light carriage, washed and polished by Tom's hand that morning, was drawn up before the door ready for Mr. Newcombe in his tallest white collar to take the reins. Tom sat beside him while Mrs. Newcombe, her fan delicately spread, her gray pompadour matching the silver of her surah silk, sat in the back seat with a complacent smile on her face as she watched her daughter take her place beside her. The new organdy dress had turned out miraculously well and in it Alice looked like a white rose with a golden crown.

The carriage moved on toward Windsor Road, which seemed almost crowded with equipages of various kinds. Even the trolley as it swung past seemed to be filled, for as Mr. Emory, the motorman, always stopped at the edge of the Adair property in any case, it was convenient for those who did not have horses to make use of this more ordinary means of transportation.

"Betsy is going to wait for me inside so we can sit together," Alice told her mother as they dismounted under the porte-cochere, crossed the great porch and entered the hall, where Miss Jenny and Miss Kitty received them with their usual soft, perfumed embrace.

"Dearest Mary, and darling Alice! It's so wonderful to see you. Do find comfortable seats. We want to remain here to greet everyone as they come."

Miss Jenny, tall, regal, in black silk and pearls, Miss Kitty, shorter, with cheeks still rosy under her white hair, her lavender voile dress trimmed with lace falling gracefully about her, turned to welcome the steady stream of incoming guests.

Betsy was already there, and she and Alice sat down near the end of the long drawing room and as usual were overcome at first by the formal elegance. The chairs and sofas were pale blue velvet, the heavy lace curtains had Honiton borders, the mantel decorations were Dresden and an alabaster statue of a water nymph stood on the end of the grand piano. Small tables with interesting bibelots were placed here and there; the rugs were Oriental and lush to the foot. Before the girls had exchanged more than a few low, nervous words, the room seemed suddenly to fill up and Molly Hart brought a few extra small chairs which she placed with their backs to the piano. After watching at the front door long enough to assure themselves there were no more late-comers, Miss Jenny and Miss Kitty, both flushed and smiling as though from inner excitement, came to stand at the doorway between drawing room and hall.

"And now," Miss Kitty began, "we have a surprise for you which we have tried to keep a secret. We have invited you all here as our closest friends to share with you a great joy which has unexpectedly come to us. Robin," she called, turning to the hall, "will you come in now, please."

There entered then the young man who had almost missed getting off the train. He was tall and held himself well but was apparently painfully embarrassed. He had wavy brown hair, blue eyes, a strong cleft chin and a fresh complexion.

Miss Jenny went on with an affectionate glance. "Sister Kitty and I wish to present a cousin from England whom we never knew we had. It was almost miraculous how he found out about us, and now we have one of our very own blood in our family, Robert Adair. It goes without saying that we call him *Robin!* Sister, won't you start the introductions on this side and I'll take over at the other end of the room. Of course," she added to the young man, "you won't remember everyone's name now but you will come to know them later."

With a graceful swish of silk petticoats under her voile Miss Kitty came over to the new relative and caught his hand for a second affectionately. Though looking miserably ill at ease he still managed to conduct himself with dignity as they began their tour of the room. He bowed stiffly but properly to the ladies and shook hands with the men. When he reached Alice his face flamed and once again he looked directly into her eyes before Miss Kitty had swept him on to the next guests. Miss Jenny completed the introductions and then suggested that everyone stand and visit a little while before they went to the dining room for refreshments, after which, she said archly, "we have another surprise for you."

In a few minutes there was general movement and conversation. The young man named Robin was plied with questions and comments and found himself drawn into the center of group after group. Once he laughed and the sound rose pleasantly above the other voices. It brought in a boyish and bouyant note in contrast to the embarrassed restraint that had marked his other utterances. Alice in the other end of the room, from whence she refused to be lured by Betsy, felt in her heart a more intimate pang of knowledge from the laugh than she had even at the second meeting of their eyes. She could see that he had made several attempts to move in her direction but each time had been stopped by interested and talkative females. Some of the remarks drifted to her.

"But do tell us how you found out about the relationship with the Miss Adairs?"

"A paper in your mother's Bible? But how romantic!"

"It seems almost miraculous, now doesn't it?"

The men, Alice noted, asked very few questions.

During refreshments, upon which Molly Hart had lavished her finest skill, the guests moved about more freely upon porch and lawn with their well-filled plates while Miss Jenny and Miss Kitty hovered solicitously among them. Twice the young man named Robin made a definite attempt to reach Alice's side and both times was blocked by George Hastings' not inconsiderable bulk. Then at last the coffee cups were passed and drained and Miss Jenny announced that all were invited back to the drawing room. Once there Alice's grandfather maneuvered a seat next to her and under cover of the confusion whispered, "He's got a good English face, the young fellow. Bowed nose, blue eyes, dimpled chin and a bulldog look to the jaws. I'll bet he could fight a wildcat if he had to and never wrinkle his suit." Alice smiled and did not answer.

Miss Jenny was standing now, awaiting attention. "Our young cousin is very modest, but we happened to discover that he sings, and after a great deal of urging has consented to sing for us tonight. Sister Kitty will accompany him. If you will come here, Robin, I think beside the piano will be the best place for you to stand."

The young man's face was red as he took the appointed spot.

David Means spoke again very low to his granddaughter. "He looks as if he'd like to go jump in a lake and I don't blame him. What a refined form of torture they're putting him through."

Then Miss Kitty rippled the keys and the voice came. A good one, untrained but a pleasing baritone. Miss Jenny read the names of the selections from a sheet of paper. "Old favorites," she explained as she announced one after another, beginning with "Drink to Me Only with Thine Eyes." When the list was finally completed Miss Kitty, always more animated than her sister, spoke from the piano seat.

"Now, *my* favorite, Robin! You know you promised. I never heard this," she added, turning to the guests, "until Robin sang it one day and now I love it. It's so sweet and rollicking. Sister Jenny feels it's almost too romantic but I know you'll like it. Come on, Robin, let's start."

A change came over the young man's face as he smiled. The smile, indeed, seemed to be in his voice when he began to sing.

"Mind you put in the Scotch words now," Miss Kitty said. Everyone in the room was sitting up a little straighter, expectantly, as the bright tune started.

> O whistle and I'll come to you, my love,
> Whistle and I'll come to you.
> Though faither and mither and all should go mad —
> Whistle and I'll come to you, my lad!
> Whistle and I'll come to you!

There was a burst of spontaneous applause when he had finished and many cries of *encore* from the men and "Oh, do sing it again!" from the ladies.

Miss Kitty beamed and nodded. "I knew they would like that, Robin, so sing it all over."

His smile was even more pronounced and his voice, amused and gay as he repeated the song. At the end, there was another round of clapping with much laughter and a general lightening of spirits. Miss Jenny, who looked as though her plans for a serious concert had gone a bit awry, accepted the new mood gracefully and suggested that the young people especially might care to see the garden now before dusk while the older folks continued their visiting here. There was immediate reaction on the part of the young guests and in a very few minutes they had all left the room and were sauntering over the porch and the front lawn. It was at this point that Robert Adair, his chin set, went straight up to Alice and asked if she would come with him to look at the rose garden. It was done quickly and quietly and in a moment they were walking off together, leaving many curious eyes behind them and George Hastings, who had been delayed by a gushing young lady, looking after them with brows drawn.

They went rather hurriedly around the house with Robin glancing often over his shoulder to be sure they were not being joined by others. When they reached the rose garden, now a mass of bloom, he relaxed somewhat and guided her to a seat along one of the paths.

"Won't you sit down," he said. "There are two things I want very much to say to you. First of all I want to ask your pardon for that day at the station. It was rude of me to stare at you so. Can you forgive me?"

"I have already forgiven you," Alice said quietly.

"Oh, thank you. That's one load off my mind. You see that day I felt so strange, so almost frightened at what I'd done, and when I looked into your eyes all at once I seemed to have found some confidence. It was more than that, of course," he added in a lower tone, "but that is all I should say, now."

"I'm glad if . . . if it helped you," Alice replied.

"But now as to the other thing. I'll speak fast, for any minute some of the others will be here. Could I come to see you? Soon? Could we meet where no one could hear the conversation? This is terribly important to me. Could you arrange this? It's about my own affairs," he added, "and I know it's a great deal to ask."

Alice sat thoughtful. There was no inviolate place in her own home. That was sure. At her grandfather's? But that might seem a little odd to Robin. At last she said slowly, "Can you paddle a canoe?"

His tense face relaxed. "Oh, yes, well enough," he answered.

"Then that would be best for a quiet talk. Would you like to come tomorrow evening? About seven? We could go down then to the creek."

"I can't thank you enough. You see, I'm terribly troubled. If I don't talk about my problem soon I think I'll lose my mind. And of all people in the world I want most to discuss it with you."

## CHAPTER TWO

W HEN THE NEWCOMBE FAMILY reached home after the soiree they all settled at once in the back parlor to talk it over. Mary Newcombe was romantically excited with nothing but complete approval of Robert Adair; Tom said he seemed a nice sort of chap and the town could stand an extra young man about his age; Alice said the party had been a charming affair; then William Newcombe laid down his cigar and spoke his mind.

"*I* think there's something fishy about this whole business. I didn't ask the young fellah any questions myself, but I heard the answers he gave to a good many others. This thing of him suddenly finding a piece of paper in his mother's Bible with the Adair girls' names on it—just after he was orphaned—now, that to me seems a little hard to swallow. Also, to leave his native country and come away over here to fifty-second cousins he'd never even heard of before and plan to *live* with them, for that's what Jenny told me he would do — well, as I say, I think there are a few things about all this that would bear investigation. And

Alice, don't you get too thick with him till we know more about him. I saw him . . ."

"Oh, so did I," his wife broke in. "He definitely singled Alice out in several ways, and Bill, I don't think you should be so suspicious. I can imagine how it could all have happened. He has no family back there now at all and the Adair girls have none here and you can see how they simply dote on him already."

"Yes," said her husband dryly, "you can certainly see that and I doubt if he's doing anything to discourage them. And Alice?"

"Yes, Father."

"Mind what I say about not getting involved with the young man."

"I certainly don't intend to get *involved*," Alice said with dignity, "but I couldn't very well refuse to let him come to call, could I? What would Miss Jenny and Miss Kitty think of me if I did that?"

"Oh, he's asked to come?" her mother said eagerly. "When?"

"Tomorrow night I told him would be convenient. I think it will be rather nice to have a change of escorts now and then."

"Well, well. If you know what you're doing. But just keep your distance for a while. I think I'll go on to bed," her father said, as he got up.

Alice and her mother talked it all over again up in her room after the downstairs was darkened for the night and Tom had followed his father's bedtime example.

"He's really so *handsome,*" Mrs. Newcombe said, "and he has such a winning sort of smile. I can't blame the Adair girls for making so much of him. But what do you suppose he's going to *do,* now that he's here?"

"I have a feeling," Alice replied slowly, "that something is troubling him and he wants to talk about it confidentially. You know if I should close the folding doors into the parlor when we're in there it would look — well, Father wouldn't like that. And if I didn't close the doors we might as well talk on the sidewalk as far as privacy is concerned. So I think we may go canoeing."

"Oh dear," her mother said as she helped remove the white organdy gown over Alice's head, "that will certainly make talk. What will George say?"

"All at once I don't care. I feel so queer, Mother. I don't know what's wrong with me. I feel happy one minute and sad the next. I really — oh I hope this doesn't sound unmaidenly — I want to see Robin tomorrow night and yet I'm sort of afraid, too. Oh, not that he's going to be sentimental or anything like that. He made it plain he just wanted to talk about his own affairs. But I hope there's nothing wrong, the way Father thinks."

"Nonsense! Your father's always imagining things. How did Grandfather like him?"

Alice laughed. "He said he had a strong jaw and he looked as if he could fight a wildcat without wrinkling his suit."

"There," Mrs. Newcombe said. "That sounds like your grandfather and he's a pretty good judge of character. Now get to bed, Alice, and have a good sleep and just let things take their course." She turned around before she left. "Wasn't that a cute song he sang at the last? Everybody liked that. I heard Miss Kitty asking him if he wouldn't whistle it, but he said he'd rather not. I'd like to have heard him. Well, now, sleep well."

There were many families who sat up late that night to discuss the big social event and especially the story of Robert Adair. Most of the women being at all ages susceptible to masculine charm agreed with Mrs. Newcombe's opinion, but a number of men shook their heads a trifle darkly and posed certain questions they would like to have answered. At last, however, the lights went out across the town except where young girls here and there stayed overnight with each other and exchanged romantic gossip until dawn.

In the great stone house on Windsor Road Miss Jenny and Miss Kitty, assisted from their dresses and silk petticoats by Molly Hart, congratulated each other all over again upon the success of the evening (and of course upon Molly's part in it) and expressed once more their delight over Robin's singing and general behavior and then went promptly and happily to sleep.

But in the Green Room, so called because the wall paper design was myrtle and ivy, the occupant of the great four-poster tossed and turned and found no rest, though he thumped his pillows, sat up at times by the window, or paced the floor. In spite of all his efforts to calm his emotional turmoil and court repose he still heard the great hall clock below chime not only the hours but the quarters as well, on and on and on. And the problem which had driven sleep from his eyes was not the one he had begged Alice Newcombe to allow him to discuss with her the next evening. This was one he could not tell to another human soul, certainly not to her. Yet. He, Robert Adair, was in love. Incredibly but utterly in love. He who had always treated girls with a light cynicism, friendly enough to many, too friendly to a few, but with a careless superiority to all, now for the first time knew the pangs from Cupid's sharp bow, himself.

He had been first amused by the song Miss Kitty had urged him to sing at the close of his little recital, for the "whistle and I'll come to you" motif had been one with which he had long been familiar in his own life. From early schooldays on into his young manhood it had, indeed, been necessary for him only to whistle (or a counterpart thereof) to have the girls come to him. Now in a pair of clear and beautiful gray eyes he had read his own male fallibility. He was no longer invincible, and so as he had ended the song he suddenly wished as he listened to the applause and laughter that he had not had to sing it. For the owner of the sweet gray eyes, no matter how gentle and kind she might seem, would come, he somehow knew, for no man's beck or call, *or whistle,* he added wryly, but only for deep and true love and along with it, respect. Thus he must try his best to achieve something of the latter, if possible, tomorrow night as he made his strange confession, all unrelated to the pain and longing in his heart.

But how suddenly this love had come! He had read of such things with amused skepticism. That his own impregnable emotions should be pierced all in a moment was shattering. He found himself trembling now as he lay in bed, with amazement, with fear, with desire. But the night was very still outside and something at last of this quiet entered the room and stole over his senses. He was conscious of the fresh breeze that comes between midnight and dawning and in it now was the scent of roses; it seemed as though a gentle spirit was abroad. In their bedrooms the sisters would be resting with the same dignity with which they presided over the great house by day; beyond them would be the faithful Molly. And somewhere not too far away, Alice Newcombe herself would be lying, her white limbs folded in slumber. It was many a year since Robert Adair had wept. Suddenly now he felt his eyes overflow. But the tears must have blessed the pain, for in the next hour, he, too, fell asleep.

The next day, in spite of a long call from Betsy, the hours dragged for Alice.

"I suppose you know," Betsy had told her, "that George is utterly furious. In the first place he thinks this Robin is a fraud and in the second place you know how jealous he is of you. I sometimes think," she added, "that even if he is my brother he has a little hard streak in him. He really *ranted* last night and that's no way to act about you when you're not even engaged yet," Betsy sighed.

"I have tried to convince George that I'm still entirely free, but he simply won't accept that."

"He may have to," Betsy answered with a side glance at her friend. "What do you really think about this Robin yourself?"

Alice's cheeks colored and she looked troubled. "I don't know," she said. "I wish I did."

And strangely the conversation foundered there when there should have been endless subjects for discussion, and before long, after trying to resume their usual chatter, they gave it up and Betsy went home.

Since it was to be a canoe ride that night instead of a steps party, Alice dressed in a plain white piqué with navy trim. Her mother put a red rose in her hair and after taking it out twice Alice put it back again just before she heard a foot fall on the sidewalk. After all, why not? The girls all wore flowers in their hair in summer and this did brighten up the dress. She tried not to suggest even in her thoughts that the rose added a piquant charm to her own beauty.

On the very moment of seven the front doorbell rang and Alice, her cheeks at the moment the color of the flower, greeted the waiting young man. He was meticulously groomed and dressed as though for boating in a soft white shirt and blue jacket. He looked down at her, smiling.

"You're very kind to let me come," he said.

"I believe, since dusk seems to fall early, we should walk on down now to the creek," she answered.

"Should I not speak to your mother?" he asked, a bit anxiously.

"Oh yes. She's right here. She wants to see you before we leave."

Mrs. Newcombe was already in the hall, and greeted the young man with a cordiality bordering upon effusion, while Alice's cheeks grew more red.

She finally reached his singing. "It was such a treat! I especially liked that last song. Where did you ever learn it?"

"Oh, when I was a boy, I guess. The young girl in it seemed to be very sure of her feelings, didn't she?"

"I never thought of that. But won't you come in and sing for us some time? Alice doesn't play too badly so she could accompany you. Won't you come?"

"Thank you. I'd love to. And don't worry about the canoe. I'll be very careful."

Alice and Robin walked under the elms and on down the path that led to the boathouse. Here several other young couples were selecting their canoes and looked up in surprise as the newcomers arrived. There were greetings, introductions and quick shoving off, as the young men displayed their dexterity with the paddles. At last only Alice and her escort were left. Also was left the choicest canoe of all with a comfortable leather covered seat for the passenger.

"We'll take this one," Robin said to the boatkeeper, and handed Alice to her place.

"Oh, this is lovely," she said, her face all smiles. "I've never been in this one before."

"Good!" he said. "Now, please be a bit patient with me for it's quite a while since I've done this. I'll probably be awkward. But at least I'll take it easy until I get the feel of it again. Meanwhile won't you talk to me. It's just occurred to me that our friendship — and I hope I can call it so — has been mainly a matter of *looking* at each other, hasn't it?"

Alice laughed and the music of it went softly over the water.

"I believe that's so. But I'm afraid I'm not very interesting as a conversationalist. The only time I seem to be full of things to say is when I'm with my grandfather. He lives in a rather quaint frame house on the edge of town and he's *wonderful,* really. I'd like to take you to call on him some time."

"I'd be proud to go."

"I could tell you about the little creek here with the Indian name. Somebody once tried to explain it. They said an Indian said, 'Cannot go in it,' and then they called it Canodoguinnett. But that's just silly. I like the Indian names for our creeks and rivers, though. It gives a nice flavor to our countryside. We have the Susquehanna and Juaniata near us and of course innumerable others all across the state. I used to know a rhyme about the Juaniata."

"Please say it for me."

Alice laughed. "It dates from my little girlhood, but I'll say what I can remember. My mother used to sing it but I forget the tune."

> Wild roved an Indian girl
> Bright Alfaretta,
> Where flowed the waters of
> The blue Juaniata;
> Swift and strong her arrows were
> In their painted quiver,
> Loose flowed her jetty locks
> A-down the rapid river.

"There," she said, "I feel silly for having repeated that. But you can see how a child would like it."

"I'm not a child, but I liked it very much. Thank you."

Then in a moment he let the canoe drift. "I've been watching that big white birch with its branches hanging over the water like a curtain. Couldn't we slip under them and be practically hidden from view and have our talk?"

Alice turned about and looked. "It's the most secluded place along the creek. Let us go."

Once there, the canoe settled comfortably beneath the branches, and the two young people stared anxiously at each other.

Robin began, laying the paddle carefully in the bottom of the boat.

"I hope you'll consider this an act of courage," he said. "I feel as though I had to make a certain confession, but I'm horribly nervous. I want above all to have your respect, and more than that I hope some day." His throat choked a little on the latter words. "So I can't cover up anything that might seem like deceit."

Alice looked at him, her gray eyes full of fright, but she did not speak.

Robin went on slowly, swallowing often. "I grew up in England, as I guess you know. My father was a bookkeeper with a small concern and a small salary. My mother died when I was fourteen and from then on he and I kept house as best we could and he taught me in the evenings, for he wanted to prepare me for a good school, you see."

He paused as though waiting for a comment, but Alice said nothing.

"When we first went through my mother's books and papers, I saw the little page of Adair genealogy. I read it but didn't pay it much attention. After my father's death I was all alone with very little money and one great ambition. I wanted to come to America. You can't imagine how I wanted to come. Over there you see I was caught in a dead end. Without my father's salary I couldn't go on to college. I got a little job as a bookkeeper and tried to save but it was pretty hopeless and I was wretched. Suddenly one day I thought of the little genealogy table which I had read years before. When I looked for it, it was gone. My father had not been interested in it and so had evidently thrown it away with other papers."

"Oh Robin," Alice said, speaking for the first time, her voice full of sympathy, "how dreadful you must have felt. Did you find it?"

"No. I wish I could say I did. The one thing I remembered distinctly was that a Miss Jane and Miss Katherine Adair, last of their line, were living at that time in Callaway, Pennsylvania, U.S.A. Even when I had first seen this the dream of coming to America was in my mind. So on the impulse I wrote with no other address, not knowing the size of the town or whether the letter would have the least chance of reaching them. Also," he stopped and mopped his forehead, "because there *had* been papers in my mother's Bible, a letter or two and a copied poem and other things, it seemed natural that this paper had been there too. In any case, without being really sure of this I said it had been. Of course I had no idea how religious the cousins were and that this would please them more than anything. From my letter they felt I had just then come upon the paper, and as they said —" he smiled wryly — " 'definitely the hand of the Lord had guided me.' "

"Oh, knowing them, they would think that," Alice said, smiling a little too.

"I pictured them as two little old spinsters probably without too much to live on and my only thought was that if I could use my bit of money to come over and have a place to stay with them for just a few weeks until I got a job I could repay them for their kindness and go on my way. But I'd be *in America!* You see I really was just using them and not being strictly honest at that. So that's why it hurts now."

For a while everything was still. Robin's face was withdrawn. Alice watched him anxiously.

"And then," she said at last, "you found everything was different."

Robin drew a long breath. "Oh," he burst out, *"different!* First of all a letter came right back enclosing money for my passage, and telling me they couldn't wait until I would come to them. They saw from my letter that I was lonely and had no relatives there, and they had none here so I must come and make their home mine, and that at last they would have one of their very own blood with them. I was utterly dumbfounded but I was also thrilled. You don't blame me for that, do you? Here was a chance better than I had ever dreamed of to get to America. So I settled my small affairs and came, thinking, I must admit, very little, indeed, about the cousins themselves, until . . ."

He stopped and his eyes met hers in a long look. "Until I was on that funny old train, bringing me into Callaway, when all at once everything swept over me. I was scared. I felt I couldn't face it all. That's why I was so long getting off. Then — I saw *you*."

Alice colored. "It was strange," she said gently, "that we really met in that way."

"But now since I have confessed everything, how do you feel about it? About me? Can you still respect me? And should I tell the cousins all I've described to you? I so want to be honest about it."

Alice's face was thoughtful and it looked as though a tear might be imminent, but when she spoke her voice was strong and firm.

"No," she said, "to the last, and yes, to the first. I respect you very much, but I think Miss Jenny and Miss Kitty should be allowed to believe just what they do now. They are *so* happy. It would be cruel to upset them in any way. They feel you are like a son to them."

"I know. It's their incredible generosity that makes it all so hard for me. I'm very fond of them but I feel as though I were being smothered between two soft, perfumed, down cushions!"

Alice threw back her head and laughed. "I know just what you mean. I love them too and they've been awfully good to me but they do almost kill you with kindness. Is there anything special that worries you?"

His face reddened. "Yes, there is. They told me they had changed their wills in my favor! Could anything make me more wretchedly uncomfortable? They're so pleased about it. Said they had no one before of their very own to leave their money to, and now they have me, so they made the changes at once. Needless to say I appreciate their thought of it but I feel miserable every time I look around and imagine what they really may be worth, even without securities. Can't you see what a position it puts me in?"

"Well," Alice said calmly, "I'm sure if I live longer than my parents my brother and I will inherit all they have, but I never give it a thought. Can't you just put it out of your mind the same way?"

"But it's not the same. You are a daughter. I'm only a *very* remote cousin and a newcomer to them at that. If they had only not *told* me! But they are as happy as children about it. They had me meet Squire Weir, who drew up the new documents. I imagined he gave me a queer look as though he thought I might have suggested the whole thing. I've done nothing wrong except what I told you in the beginning but somehow I feel like a cad. If the word of this should get out over the town I wouldn't blame people for thinking I'm a sort of fortune hunter. And on top of everything else I want to get a *job*. I want to go to work and they constantly hold me back. They insist that I wait until a 'position worthy of the name' comes up. But how can it when I'm staying around the house all the time? We have a slow late breakfast and then they like me to supervise this Charles, the gardener, who I may add doesn't *like* any supervision even if I knew how to give it. Then there is a long slow lunch, then they take naps, then Molly Hart sets out the tea things and I always help her for the sake of something to do."

"That's good of you. Does anyone come to tea?"

"Oh, heavens yes. All the old ladies in town drop in and I have to *sing* for them! I tell you, Alice, I don't know how long I can keep this up. And yet . . ."

"You're sorry for them," Alice said gently.

"That's it. I can see they've been terribly lonely. Molly Hart isn't exactly what you'd call a 'blithe spirit.' "

Alice giggled. "Not exactly."

"And I've never had the chance before to make anyone so happy as they are now. So I feel I've got to stick it out a while longer and do my best for them. Do you see any ray of hope for me?"

Alice nodded emphatically. "There's one person that ought to hear the whole story. That's my grandfather. This is a big secret I'm about to tell you and half of it is guessed at. But years ago, I think he was very fond of Miss Jenny and I believe he wouldn't marry her because he was afraid of getting into a situation a little like you're in now. At any rate I'm sure he would understand your position and he just might have an idea about a job. He's always been a student on the side but his real work has been in business. I've no idea how much but I have a feeling he's made a good deal of money. My father says he's *shrewd,* but I wouldn't use that word except in a nice way about him. I'm pretty fond of him and I'd like you to meet him soon."

"You don't know how much I want to. By *soon,* do you mean tomorrow or next week, or what?"

Alice considered. "Do you ever use the horses there?"

"I have a few times."

"Then why not ask for the use of the surrey tomorrow afternoon while the sisters are having their naps. You could tell them you were going to take me for a drive . . . I think they would be . . . I mean they might . . . you see they rather . . ."

"Yes," Robin smiled as she floundered and blushed. "They have made it quite plain how highly they think of you. I'm sure they would approve of the drive. Almost as much as I would," he added. "When should I stop for you?"

"Now this is where I must use a little subterfuge," she said. "You see my father has certain ideas about my seeing too much of any strange young man."

"Meaning me."

"So, I will just walk over to Grandfather's as I always do, maybe even have lunch with him, which will give me time to sketch in your problem a little before you come. Would you mind that?"

"You know I would be eternally grateful."

"Then you can have a good talk later on and afterwards it would be very natural for you to take me for a little drive, wouldn't it?"

"You're a born diplomat. And a great deal more," he said quietly. "Does it matter that it has grown dark upon us here?"

"Mercy yes!" Alice exclaimed. "We must get out into the open at once. I love my town but as Grandfather says, its bricks are cemented by gossip which has an unpleasant way of hardening sometimes."

It took a bit of doing to get the canoe off the reedy bottom, but it shot out at last, and Robin guided it slowly and casually down the stream among the last boaters and then back to the landing dock. He helped Alice out, paid for the canoe and was starting with her up the path from the creek when a large form blocked their way. It was George Hastings.

"Hello, George," Alice said a little nervously. "I think you've met Robin Adair."

"I've met him all right," George hissed, "and I've a few words to say to him. I want to tell you, Adair, to keep your hands off my girl."

Robin stared at him for a long second, astonished, then he said quietly, "In the first place, Hastings, I didn't know you had the right to call her *your girl,* and in the second, I have certainly never laid my hands upon her. So let's get the thing straight."

"And that's what I mean to do," George went on, taking a step nearer. "There are some things you ought to know and everybody is too mollycoddle to tell you. This whole town thinks you're a dirty, fortune-hunting rat and that you've taken in the Miss Adairs with a cock and bull story that nobody could believe and that the sooner you . . ."

He did not finish the sentence for an arm shot out and George Hastings suddenly fell over backwards and lay sprawling, dazed and panting in the moist dirt.

"We'd better go on, Alice," Robin said, taking her arm.

"Will he be . . . be all right?"

"Oh, sure. When he gets his wind. I'm sorry it happened though. It's not a nice thing to fight in front of a lady but I couldn't let him call me those names and do nothing."

"Of course you couldn't."

There was no more conversation until they were almost at the Newcombes' house, then Robin said, as though the question was a painful one. "I should have asked you sooner. Are you really, as Hastings said, *his girl?*"

"I am not," she answered promptly. "We've been going together for a good while and he seemed to assume that this made things settled between us but *I* never felt so, and he never once put any of his feelings into words. He's a very *cautious* young man," she added, with the hint of a laugh in her voice.

"Thank you. The evening has been wonderful and I feel as though my burden is a lot easier since you've been kind enough to listen to my troubles. Oh, and please tell me how I get to your grandfather's house tomorrow."

She told him in detail, they shook hands and he thanked her once more after she reached her own doorway. He turned, however, before she entered, and ran back up the steps.

"Maybe I should warn you," he said smiling, "that I'm not a *cautious* young man."

Mrs. Newcombe showed a little disappointment in the report of the canoe ride, but aside from explaining that Robin was concerned about having no job as yet and not knowing how to go about finding one, Alice gave no details. One thing she dreaded. There had been others on the bank of the creek who would have witnessed the fight, if such it could be called, and it would not take long for the whole town to learn of it. Worst of all those who saw George sprawled in the mud by the quick blow would not have been near enough to hear the words which had caused it.

"I think tomorrow," Alice was saying, "I may make a little visit to Grandfather. Do you mind if I have lunch with him?"

"Well, of course not," her mother answered, looking at her keenly. "Maybe you'll tell him what you haven't told me. That's all right, though I do feel I should have your full confidence too. I like young Adair and if you intend to go right on seeing him often you'd better hang on to me as an ally, for your father gets awfully set in his opinions."

Alice laughed and kissed her mother. "Now please don't be huffy. Of course I'll tell you more later but I would like to get Grandfather's opinion on some things first. All right?"

"Have to be, I guess. But ask the young man to come up some time and sing for us. Oh, I think that's your father now. He's been at a meeting. You'd better hurry on up to bed, Alice."

But it proved to be Tom who came in as though blown through the door by the wind. He looked from his mother in the hall to his sister halfway up the stairs and burst out with his news.

"So the quiet old town is getting some life in it. What did you think of the fight, Mother?"

"The *what?*"

"Your daughter didn't tell you?"

"No," Mrs. Newcombe said tartly, "she didn't."

"Well then, I'll have the pleasure. Our new friend, Robert Adair, gave George Hastings a good sock, and sent him flying."

"In front of you, Alice?" Mrs. Newcombe exclaimed in horror. "What possessed Adair to do such a terrible thing?"

"Well, the fellows all say it was because Hastings didn't like Adair's being with you, Sis," Tom began, when Alice stopped him.

"That wasn't it at all. Did George not tell the real reason Robin hit him?"

"Not any more than that."

Alice's cheeks were flaming. "Well, I'll tell you. He called Robin a dirty fortune-hunting rat who had taken the Miss Adairs in with a cock and bull story no one in town believed and . . ."

Tom whistled. "Whew!" he said. "Good for Adair. I'd have done the same thing he did. George has been strutting round here a little too much if you ask me, and maybe it won't hurt him to be brought down a peg. The only thing . . ."

He stopped, eyeing his sister. "You might tell Adair to be a little on the lookout. George says he's going to get even if it's the last thing he does."

"But that's dreadful," Alice replied. "Robin will never have a minute's peace. It's not *fair!*" Her voice rose on the word.

"What's not fair?" her father said, coming in the door.

There was a second's silence and then Tom said as casually as he could, "Oh, George Hastings made a pretty ugly remark to Robert Adair and got a punch on the nose. Now George is breathing out threatenings and slaughter but I don't imagine there will be any more of it."

"You saw this, Tom?"

"No, I just heard about it from the other fellows."

"Well, now, I have this to say." Mr. Newcombe assumed his most pontifical air. "George Hastings is a fine, upstanding young man whom we've known all his life. We know his family. We know his prospects, which seem to be very good. He's been coming round here in what I would call a courting mood for nearly a year and I do not wish to see him humiliated by any young fly-by-night upstart, and I must warn you, Alice . . ."

"Oh, Father, I'll be *most* discreet," Alice said, as she flew up the stairs and closed her bedroom door forcibly behind her. Once there she buried her face in the pillows and wept. For a new and heavy weight oppressed her, an omen, a prescience. She knew now that the strange unsettled yearning in her heart was love. But she knew, too, that it lay upon her like an incubus, a burden of what was to come. She foresaw for the first time in her glad, carefree, girlish years the conflict between the possibilities and the actualities of life. She was sure from the few words he had said and all he had carefully refrained from saying that Robin loved her also, but she could not shake off the feeling that an undefined danger threatened them.

She put the light out quickly and undressed in the dark, for she felt she couldn't discuss the matter further just then with her mother. But later, lying wakeful in bed, she decided that it was equally hard to be alone, and started up once to call for companionship. She desisted, however. The best solace would be to tell the whole story to her grand-father.

The next morning was all sunshine streaming down from a cloudless sky. Alice, having overslept, jumped up quickly, ran to the window to drink deeply of the mild air scented from the garden below, then drew a breath of relief. What could have been the matter with her last night? How silly all her dark forebodings seemed now! Why, she was in love! Robin was in love with her. What a miracle! What a blessed, happy miracle! As to George Hastings, who had really been the cause of her anxiety, she might just have a little talk with him herself and clear things up once and for all. As she dressed her voice rose in an old song which seemed to suit the weather.

> Fair as the morning,
> Bright as the day;
> Visions of beauty
> Tarry for aye.

When she entered the dining room she found the men gone but Mrs. Newcombe ready to sit down to a second cup of coffee.

"Well, you sound in fine fettle this morning," the latter said aggrievedly. "I must say after all that happened last night you seem to have shed it very quickly. I think you were definitely *compromised*."

"Oh, Mother, we all made too much of it. What I

really want most is for Grandfather to hear everything and then I'll tell you all he says. He always has a better perspective on things than we do."

"Perspective or not I don't think he'll like the idea of two young men fighting over his granddaughter."

"But it wasn't that, really."

"You can't tell me," said Mrs. Newcombe. "Why don't you take young Adair out to Father's and let him do his own explaining?"

Alice blushed slowly and completely. "That's just what I'm going to do."

Her mother stared at her in amazement.

"Alice Newcombe!" she pronounced. "I do believe you're in love with him. And this time I stand with your father. For heaven's sake, go slow. I'm afraid for you."

Alice rose from the table with a light laugh. "How can I come to any harm going to Grandfather's? And do please give me credit for a little common sense."

She kissed her mother, told her the details of the plan, and then catching up her hat, went out through the kitchen.

"And I won't be late," she called, pausing to pat Sally Ann. "We'll probably be on the steps tonight."

The warm summer sun brought out the perfume from the sweet peas on their trellis and the early phlox and late lilies from the garden beds. Alice drank it in pleasurably as she hurried toward the tall wooden gate at the foot of the lot. By this means she could emerge unseen from the front street and escape the possible eyes of Betsy who might be on her way down. It was odd that she had heard nothing from her all morning, unless George had told his side of the story and Betsy had believed it. After all, he *was* her brother. Alice sighed as she felt the weight on her heart again and almost ran to the end of the street where the quiet road upon which her grandfather lived seemed to envelop her with peace. She slowed her pace, and looked about her. He had bought a wide stretch of land surrounding his house and planted it years ago according to his taste so there was now a fair-sized orchard and a good pasture field to lend a gentle pastoral quality to the scene. In the midst of this stood the white frame dwelling with its gingerbread trimming and commodious porch, all bathed now in a sunny silence.

"I think Robin will like this," she kept repeating to herself; but the real problem was how to prepare her grandfather for his guest? How much should she tell him beforehand? When she reached the porch with the wisteria vine twined around its wooden pillars she shed her trepidation. The old gentleman, hair and moustache neatly trimmed, cheeks rosy and eyes keen and quizzical, sat in his favorite chair with the wide writing arm, and smiled at the girl before him.

"*So!*" he began. "I was right about our young soloist. He didn't have to wrestle with a wildcat but I hear he did pretty well with George Hastings!"

"Oh, Grandfather," Alice said, aghast, as she kissed him. "This is what I've come to tell you and . . . how in the world do you just sit here away back on this woods road and find out everything yourself?"

"Oh, not myself," David Means grinned. "I have an emissary. You know Hepsy has been my housekeeper for twenty years or so. Every morning she rushes through the kitchen work, puts on her white apron and her white sunbonnet, takes her basket and starts out to shop. By the time she gets back . . . oh my! Outside of how many times any man may have kissed his wife she is then prepared to give me the complete news of the town." He stared off thoughtfully. "I'll not deny that it does diversify my quiet morning hours. What made young Adair take a swipe at Hastings? Not that I disapprove of it," he added.

Alice giggled and then grew very sober indeed. "I thought maybe I could have lunch with you and give you some of the details while we ate and then, Grandfather . . ." She paused with a little flush. "I have been very presumptuous but it's only because I love you so much."

"Sly little flatterer! Well, go on."

"I've invited Robin to come up here later and tell you his problems himself. For he's got some pretty big ones."

"I wouldn't be surprised. Not at all," he said thoughtfully. "Well, I'll listen with a sympathetic ear, though I don't know whether I can be of any help. I liked the cut of the young fellow's jib right away and my instinct would be to trust him with anything. Except my granddaughter," he added. "For the first and only time in my life I agree with your father. Go slow, Alice. This Adair's a stranger. He's got to prove himself. The circumstances under which he turned up here, while I'm not of a suspicious nature, could perhaps bear a bit of explanation."

"But that's just what he's coming to do, what I've begged him to do."

David Means laid a gentle finger on Alice's cheek. "Don't blush so, dearie. It's most becoming but it scares me a little. I imagine lunch is ready. Hepsy will have seen you come in and be eager to get out here and hear the conversation as she sets the table. Ah, yes, here she comes!"

Hepsy was tall and gaunt with elbows that always seemed akimbo even when hanging at her sides. She had sharp rather bold eyes and dark hair which she wore brushed back as though by fierce strokes of the brush. Her mouth was large and kind, however, giving the lie to the narrow forehead and beady eyes. When she looked upon David Means her rather hard face softened. Her one great friend was Molly Hart and as they took a stroll together of an evening, smiles often followed them. For physically they could not have been more diverse, except for their common lack of beauty. Molly was short and over plump. Her eyes were a bashful faded blue that always seemed to be searching for something; her hair was put up in curlers each night in the vain hope of ringlets in the morning.

They had two strong psychological bonds. They were both lonely and unfulfilled, Hepsy bitterly resigned, Molly still drowned in hopes and longings. The other bond was their abject devotion to their employers.

Hepsy came out to the porch now, bearing the lunch cloth and napkins. Alice was one of her favorites so she gave her a warm welcome.

"I've got a souffle for you if it hasn't fallen flat," she said. "These here fancy cheese things I don't hold with, but we'll see. Mr. Means, here, likes them."

4994

"And so do I," Alice said. "You know yours are always perfect. Oh, I'm glad I got here for lunch."

"It was in my teacup this morning you'd be comin'," Hepsy stated with conviction. "*A guest,* it read and who would it be but you?"

When all was ready the soufflé as usual was found to be perfect, and after a few leading questions which Alice parried, Hepsy returned to the kitchen. Mr. Means laid his book aside, saying he had found a treasure and he'd have to ask young Adair about it and then Alice sketched in the highlights of Robin's problems, omitting the matter of the will. She had a feeling that it was a man's subject. Her grandfather smiled often over her account but ended by looking grave.

"Yes, a queer life for an active young man. I fear he'll bolt if he doesn't get some relief soon. One thing in his favor is that he doesn't *like* the situation. If he did, he'd be lost. Has he met Squire Weir?"

"Oh, yes. He drops in often for tea."

"I'll bet he does," Mr. Means said. "He has always had a good nose for sweet things."

"You dislike him, Grandfather?"

"Oh, not as bad as that. I just wish the sisters wouldn't consult him like a lawyer and tell him all their secret affairs. What the squire knows today, the town knows tomorrow."

"Oh, dear," Alice said with a worried look, "that's not good, is it?"

"Not exactly. He's a sissified old gossip, to put it in plain

English, and how he does love other people's business! Well, I guess he can't do them any harm. When is the young man coming?"

"Soon, I'm sure. And Grandfather, I didn't tell you all his worries. He may want to explain some of them himself. Just be . . ."

"Kindly disposed toward him, eh? Well, I can promise you that."

When Robin finally arrived at the porch after tying the horses to the ring in the tall upping block outside, he showed acute embarrassment in spite of David Means's efforts to put him at ease. After a few minutes the old gentleman picked up the book he had mentioned to Alice.

"You're an Englishman," he said to Robin, "have you ever run across Gilbert White's *Selborne?*"

"I'm afraid not, sir."

"Well, this man went to a little town as a young parson and spent his life there, studying the natural history of the place on the side, and setting down his findings in beautiful prose. It's now a classic. I've only come on it lately myself and this morning I found a passage that sent me chuckling. Listen to this: 'My musical friend at whose house I am now visiting has tried all the owls that are his neighbors with a pitch pipe set at concert pitch, and finds they all hoot in B flat.' What do you think of that?"

For answer Robin suddenly relaxed, threw his head back and laughed until he was breathless.

"That's the funniest thing I ever heard in my life!" he gasped. "Thank you for reading me that."

"Since you're musical I thought it might appeal to you. Well, now, let's get down to what's on your mind. Alice has told me a little. I will be glad to help you if I can, especially since you like the owl episode. Suppose you start at the beginning."

"I didn't tell him about the wills, Robin."

*"The wills!"* Mr. Means's eyes narrowed sharply. "On second thought I believe you'd better begin with that. What do you know of their wills?"

"It's really been my biggest worry. Miss Jenny and Miss Kitty called me into the parlor one day, both looking very happy. This Squire Weir was already there."

"The devil he was," Mr. Means said softly.

"They explained then that they had just changed their separate wills in my favor since I was their own relative. I thought this Squire Weir looked a little grim as he watched me. He kept saying, 'Now Miss Jenny, you're sure this is what you want. And you, Miss Kitty?' And they both said it was so wonderful to feel their possessions would go to one of their own name and blood. But you can imagine how uncomfortable this makes *me* feel, sir."

"I can," said Mr. Means dryly. "I can, indeed. They should have kept quiet, but they are a pair of sweet blessed old idiots when it comes to anything relating to money. Do you have any idea what was in their former wills?"

Robin looked startled. "Why no. Not the slightest. How would I?"

"Oh, it would be quite in keeping with their innocent natures to have the squire compare the new will with the old.

In your presence," he added. "The thing that bothers me most is that the squire is not a . . . a *reticent* man, to use an understatement."

Robin smiled, even though his eyes looked anxious.

"And there's nothing we can do about that?"

"The only thing as I see it is for you to put the business of the wills out of your mind and then lead as normal a life here as possible. But you must have a job."

"If I don't soon get one, I'll have to bolt," the young man said grimly.

"Exactly. Now it's possible I can help you here, though it won't be anything thrilling. I've always liked to have my finger in a good many pies, so while the Miss Adairs own the carpet factory I'm on the board of directors and since we've been such old friends they listen to me. Then . . . do you know anything about a hardware store?"

"Not much, though I've always liked the smell of one."

Mr. Means chuckled. "So did I from a boy on, so I bought this one for myself."

"Why, Grandfather!"

"Sh . . . it's a secret in a way. But this is a big concern. They sell everything from kitchen gadgets to plows and harrows and sleighs and so on. And right now they need a bookkeeper. Alice tells me you are one."

"My father was, and he taught me quite a little. I'm just fair but I can keep books."

"The logical place for you is in the carpet factory but there are two problems. We already have a good bookkeeper there and also this Hastings whom I hear you met again yesterday . . ." he paused while they all laughed, "is doing pretty well in retail and you might have to be under him."

"I will take the hardware store if I can get it and the cousins approve."

"They won't," Mr. Means said, "but I'll talk to them. I'll invite myself to dinner tomorrow night, and Alice, couldn't you invite Robin so he'll be out of the way and I think have a livelier time at that. And now, young man, just run quickly over the details of how you came to be here. Right from the beginning, please."

As he listened, Mr. Means never took his eyes from Robin's face, keen eyes, appraising eyes they were, which missed nothing, allowed for no loophole. At the end he stood up as he always did when he felt a visit should be terminated, and held out his hand.

"A strange, a queer story," he said, "but I find it entirely credible. Alice's advice has been good. Follow it and count on me to help you in any way I can. By the way, were you always called *Robin?*"

"Good heavens no. My nickname was Rob. It was the cousins who at once felt that because of the song I should be Robin. Here again they were so pleased I couldn't bear to hurt them, but I do feel like a fool, except . . ." He stopped and looked at the girl. "I must say I like hearing it from Alice."

Mr. Means smiled tenderly. "Yes, she turns everything to favor and to prettiness as the poet says. But I think you'll have to keep on being Robin for a while for the old ladies' sake. Hold your head up, forget the will business, I'll try to get you a temporary job and we'll see how things work out. One thing I must say," and his face was suddenly very grave. "Take good care of my granddaughter."

Robin returned the gravity. "You can rest assured of that, sir. And thank you again for the owls."

He untied the horses, handed Alice into the surrey, sprang in himself and with much waving of hands they drove off.

David Means stood at the steps looking after them, slowly shaking his head. He spoke softly to himself.

"I think they're in love," he murmured, "and I like that boy. Unqualifiedly. There's something intensely honest about him, and of course in any girl's eyes he would have charm. I can't explain why I trust him, but I do. Only . . ." he looked off at the surrey retreating under the trees along the country road. "It's all such a queer setup. I feel just a little disturbed."

# Chapter Three

TOM'S STATEMENT that new life seemed to have entered the old town proved to be true. During the next weeks there could be felt in the staid and quiet streets a small tremor of romantic excitement. Some things of course remained the same. The young ladies, under their parasols, still strolled along the station platform at six o'clock when the Old Girl came puffing sedately along the tracks. Matrons in the vicinity watched to see who had been up to the county seat for shopping or who else was starting on down the valley for visits here and there. There were still steps parties, canoeing and trolley rides for the young, all with a subtle difference. And this difference was produced by the presence of Robin Adair.

In the big stone house where Miss Jenny and Miss Kitty lived, the change had been more than subtle, it had been, for a time, all but volcanic. David Means, as good as his word, had invited himself to dinner one evening and appeared at his most handsome and ingratiating best to direct the old ladies' minds along the way he wished them to go while

Robin was out with Alice. After dinner and the usual reminiscences and chitchat Mr. Means came to the point.

"I like your young man. This Robin."

"Oh, who could help it?" said Miss Jenny. "He's simply brightened our lives. We can't do enough for him. We've even changed our wills in his favor. Don't you think that's nice?"

"That depends," said Mr. Means. "But if I were you I wouldn't talk about that. Wills are a secret business. Since you've brought it up, though, how did the squire react to this? Does he stand to lose because of it if he should outlive you?"

"Well," said Miss Kitty ingenuously, "he does but he said it didn't matter at all. He has plenty really with his stationery store and there was always money in the Weir family, you know. He's quite well fixed. We give him something each time he comes out to help or advise us in any way and we have decided from now on to give him more. So he's perfectly satisfied."

David Means naturally did not voice the profane words aloud but to himself he was thinking, *Like hell, he is.* "And Molly Hart," he spoke suddenly. "Any change there?"

"No," Miss Jenny said firmly. "She is still well provided for." Then she added, "I know you, David Means. You've got something on your mind. That's why you came out tonight. Do tell us. Is it something about Alice Newcombe? You know Kitty and I are watching . . . we're so interested . . . we have a feeling . . ."

"So have I," he smiled, "but that's not my errand. I think

among us we've got to scare up a job for this young man or he'll leave."

*"Leave!"* they whispered in one terrified breath. "Why would he want to *leave?* We do everything for him," Miss Kitty said, her face pale.

"Well, maybe that's the trouble. You both, and I too, are old people. He is young and active and thank heaven wants to do a man's work. Don't you see that he can't go on staying here doing nothing but entertaining you no matter how fond he is of you?"

"David, you amaze me. There are plenty of young men who never hold *jobs,* as you call them, if they have private means. They live as *gentlemen.* And what," she added abruptly, "could he ever find to do in this town that would be worthy of his talents?"

David sat as in deep concentration before speaking. "He knows how to keep books, which might do for a starter. But at the carpet factory now, we have a good man doing that."

"Oh, *never* the carpet factory. To give him a position there would seem like . . . oh, you know that ugly word that means favoring your relatives."

"Nepotism?" David Means prompted.

"Yes. What a nasty sound it has. Well, that's out."

"Then," David went on, "there is the hardware store, which in the last years has become really big business. There is a large addition now, you know, for farm machinery and that's profitable."

"You must be joking," Miss Kitty said. "To think of our Robin, going off each day to work in a hardware store! Imagine telling *that* to our friends!"

"The office has a separate entrance now and I selected good furniture for it. Henry Ross was our bookkeeper there for years but he's retired from ill health. No one ever looked down on him, certainly."

"Oh no," Miss Jenny said slowly. "His mother was a Mc-Bane. All his family connections were good."

"And he was an elder in the church," Miss Kitty added.

"Well then. What are you fussing about? If Robin would accept this position he would be following a man of some prominence in the town, and as I said . . ."

"Yes," Miss Jenny pounced. "That just now struck me. Why did *you* select the office furniture?"

"Because," David said, eyeing the ceiling, "I happen to own the store. But please don't mention it. I bought it twenty-odd years ago when it was going down hill and I've had some fun building it up."

"Then if Robin took this . . . this *job,* you would be in a position to oversee him a little?"

"I certainly would."

"Of course," Miss Jenny said thoughtfully, "that would make a difference." Then she wiped her eyes. "But oh, our routine here would be completely disrupted. Just when we're so happy."

"He would likely have to leave before our breakfast," Miss Kitty said with a small sob, "and perhaps could not get back till late afternoon and then if he went out in the evenings with the young people . . . Oh, I think this will just break our hearts."

"Now, now," said David Means. "It will not be all that bad. The other young men I know go to work and yet see a great deal of their families. Have your lunch at a time that would suit him, and he could come out on the trolley. He'll be here weekends and I'm sure he doesn't go out every night. Now, brace up. If this goes through, you'll have a happy, contented guest in the house instead of a restless one. And listen. Tomorrow afternoon have your man drive you into town and stop by the hardware store. I'll be waiting at the door marked *Private* and take you into the office. You'll feel different then. I'm really rather proud of it."

After he left that evening Miss Kitty said, "Do you really think David knows what he's talking about?"

"He usually does," Miss Jenny answered. "That's what makes it difficult to argue with him. Well," with a long sigh, "even if Robin is gone all day, it will be better than losing him altogether. I don't think I could stand that, really."

"Nor I," echoed Miss Kitty.

The next afternoon after their nap period, Charles, the gardener, coachman and general handyman, brought the light surrey to the door and the ladies, in gray suits as befitted a business occasion, stepped in and rode to town. David Means was on hand to help them out before the door marked *Private* next to the store itself. He led them then through a short paneled hall to the office at the end. Here, Miss Jenny and Miss Kitty sank down on comfortable leather chairs and looked about them in amazement. David had indeed spared neither money nor effort in furnishing the small sanctorum. The floor was hardwood with a muted Oriental in the center; the large desk and smaller table were both polished mahogany; the two engravings on the walls were masculine and seemly: one of Washington crossing the Delaware, and one a panel of the heads of hunting dogs. The back window, giving a view of the Canodoguinnett Creek, had bookshelves bordering it.

"I am always running short of book room," David explained apologetically, "so I bring some down here. As a matter of fact this is in a sense *my* office. I like to have a spot near the center of things where I can check the business. But if your Robin will come here, I won't bother him. I have a feeling we would get on together. Well, what do you think?"

Miss Jenny at last found her voice. "David, this puts an entirely different face on the whole matter. Any young man, if he worked at all, would be proud to work in an office like this. Will we speak to him about the . . . ah . . . position, or will you?"

"I will, if you don't mind. I know all its phases better, perhaps."

"And we'll break the news to Molly about the changes in our meal times. Poor girl! She'll be *so* disappointed, for Robin always helped her set out the tea things and she said it just made the day for her to have him so kind."

David's eyes narrowed a trifle. "Oh, she did? Well," he ended rather enigmatically, "things may work out for the best in many ways."

In two weeks' time the apparent volcanic changes in the stone house had settled into a new and livable routine. Breakfast was now at eight with the sisters usually in trailing negligees and lace caps over their white pompadours.

Robin could then be at his desk by nine while they performed their post-breakfast toilettes at leisure. Lunch was promptly at one and Robin came back for it. There was a noticeable change in him when he reached home in the late afternoon. He was brim full of vivacity. He laughed, he told the sisters any jokes he had heard suitable for their ears, he tore up and down stairs as though bursting with high spirits, and whether he was going out after dinner or not he willingly sang their favorite songs for them, always ending, by request, with "Whistle and I'll Come to You, My Love."

While the sober monotony of their days had been brightened immeasurably by Robin's coming in the first place, the sisters now admitted to themselves that unselfishness paid in the end. If they had not agreed to what had seemed disruption of their newly arranged lives, they would not have known this tremendous young thrill of vitality which seemed to shake the very stones of the house itself and find its way from Robin's heart to their own.

Only Molly Hart kept outside the circle of delight. She wept often when she thought no one was near. Miss Kitty saw the tears one day and spoke in distress.

"Why Molly! Whatever is the matter?"

"Nothing," Molly said stubbornly.

"But there is. You must tell me. I demand to know."

"It's just that things ain't the same." She gave a small sob. "You mebbe didn't know, but he often dried the lunch dishes for me and he always helped me at tea time, and everything's different now."

"I know, Molly. We've had to change our way of living a little and we all miss him through the day but you mustn't take it so to heart. Just look how much happier he seems to be now since he's working, and he'll be here all the time on weekends."

"It won't be the same then," Molly said doggedly and turned to her work.

Though questioned again she would add no more. "It just ain't like it was," she would repeat.

Miss Jenny spoke guardedly to Robin one afternoon before dinner. "It's about Molly," she began. "I'm afraid she's quite unhappy."

"Why, what's wrong with Molly?" he asked in surprise.

"Well, you see, our home here was very quiet before you came and I realize now that Molly's days were quite monotonous for a young woman, so small things meant much to her like your helping her set out the tea things, for instance. I just wondered if you could be specially kind to her now?"

Robin's wise young eyes looked into Miss Jenny's innocent old ones for a moment. Then he said, "I'll try to be extra jolly when she's around and I'll praise her cooking often. How would that be?"

"That would help I'm sure. Her great friend is Hepsy, Mr. Means's housekeeper, and they go for walks in the evenings. I suppose you couldn't happen to meet them some night and walk just a very little way with them? That would please them both enormously."

Robin smiled. "I'm not sure I could work that out," he said, "but I'll do the best I can here."

"Are you going out tonight?"

"I was intending to go to a steps party at Alice Newcombe's if it's all right with you and Miss Kitty."

Miss Jenny smiled and dimpled. "Of course! You see, Robin, we are so . . . so *fond* of Alice."

He looked to see that no one was entering the room, then he cupped her ear with his hands and whispered, "So am I." After which he kissed her and ran whistling up the stairs.

It had been a good many weeks since there had been as elaborate a steps party as Alice had arranged for that night. The weather was perfect, pleasant warmth after a scorching week; the moon was full; not one but two large layer cakes stood on the kitchen table, with pitchers of lemonade nearby ready for the chipped ice. Tom spread the red carpet strip early; Alice arranged the cushions. Both brought extra camp chairs from the garden to place against the house at the side of the steps and all was ready.

Alice's heart was beating uncomfortably fast as it always did at the thought of seeing Robin. She would not admit it too frankly even to herself, but this party was in reality a little celebration for him and his new job. Her grandfather had spoken of the matter in what was very high praise for him.

"That young man is all right, Alice. He's clever and keen and can stick to his business. He's caught some mistakes already that would have cost us money. I drop in once in a while for a chat."

"Oh, Grandfather, I'm *so* glad you like him," Alice had answered with the color rising in her cheeks.

"Well, keep your feelings in hand. I was just remarking he was a good bookkeeper."

To Alice's relief Betsy had returned to their usual friendly status, and in a way, more important still, George had made no further antagonistic move. Tom reported that the fellows all thought he had now left the field to Robin.

"Whatever that means," Alice had retorted with some spirit.

Tom had laughed. "Think it over, Sis, and you just might get the idea."

As a matter of fact Robin left no doubt as to his preference. He took Alice canoeing, and for drives in the evenings, and when there was a trolley or a steps party, he managed to sit close beside her.

On this early September evening the air was sweet with the last of summer and the first of autumn's fragrance; the great golden hunter's moon sailed serenely over the southern sky and as the guests arrived the talk and laughter seemed to instill in the twilight a gradual cadence of youth and happiness, for hearts were light and the hours stretching ahead were all freely their own. It was a large party. By the time the last guests had come every seat was filled. The usual irrepressible fun and jokes began at once.

"Here's a good one I just heard," Sandy Low began. "There was a farmer lived out here a little ways and he had this daughter . . ."

"Hold it!" Tom said firmly. "Not that one. There are ladies present."

Sandy stood up and solemnly surveyed the group. "Where?" he asked, mystified.

This was received with hilarity and cries from the girls of, "Oh Sandy, you're a *caution!*"

Other pointless if acceptable witticisms followed; there

was gossip of the town, discussion of Robin's new job and then, as if by common consent, the singing started. There were good voices in the group and the old harmonies rolled pleasantly along the quiet street.

"Now, the *Whistle* song," the girls begged. Most of the young people knew it by now. In fact it had become a sort of motif among them, so Robin obligingly led off and the others joined in:

> Whistle and I'll come to you, my lad!
> Whistle and I'll come to you.

At the end Alice looked appealingly at Robin. "You must know ever so many more of the lighter songs," she said. "I've heard about the English music halls. Aren't they a little like what is called vaudeville over here?"

"Somewhat, I imagine," he said smiling down at her.

"Couldn't you sing us some of the songs you've heard there?"

Robin looked at Tom. "Censorship needed?" the latter said laughing.

"With some," Robin answered. "Not with all. Well, here's an old favorite I'll try for you. It's pure Cockney and you may not understand it all. For instance, 'Knocked 'em in the old Kent Road' doesn't mean he hit them. He just — how do you say it? — Knocked their eye out. Well, here goes."

His audience was delighted and above all, praised his mastery of what they called another *language*.

"At least another dialect," Betsy said, "and oh, please, another."

Robin looked again at Tom. "There's a funny one about an old woman who had too much to drink but I don't think it's objectionable."

"Go ahead."

So Robin sang:

> And so they carried Carrie to the ferry
> And the ferry carried Carrie to the shore;
> And the reason that they had to carry Carrie
> Was that Carrie couldn't carry any more.

When the song ended the boys laughed uproariously and while there was a hesitant question or two from the girls, it was put down as a great success.

"We don't want to impose on you, Robin," Alice said, "but *would* you sing just one more very funny one. We've never heard any of these, you know. Would you? It's a treat for us."

Robin sat close to her on the outer edge of the upper step. He looked into her sweet gray eyes and knew he could refuse her nothing, now or ever.

"Just one more then," he said. "This is one I used to sing as a boy to the tune of 'My Grandfather's Clock,' and I warn you it's utterly crazy." He began:

> My grandfather's whiskers were too large for his face,
> So they grew round the brim of his hat . . .

This, when finished, was pronounced the best yet, and Alice, standing up, said she thought everyone was just in the right mood for refreshments. Betsy and Tom rose too and she nodded shyly to Robin so with the efforts of the four, the plates of cake and glasses of lemonade were soon circulated. It was when the repast had ended with much praise that a tall form was seen approaching. A cloud had drifted momentarily across the moon, and the early twilight seemed suddenly to have the substance of night.

"It's my brother," Betsy whispered to Alice. "He said he wasn't coming."

But he came straight to the middle of the group.

"Hello, George," Tom called. "You just missed the cake. Is there a piece left, Alice?"

"Of course," she said, starting to rise, but George stopped her by a gesture and came over to the end of the step where she sat next to Betsy with Robin on the far side.

George's voice had a raucous sound in the quiet air. With an unexpected movement he gave a shove against Betsy which sent her against Alice and Robin off the step entirely. He jumped up quickly, stood a moment as though collecting himself and then sat down where the girls made his former place for him. It was Tom who spoke angrily above the low growls of the other boys.

"That was a mean trick, George," he began. "What possessed you to do it? The girls might have been hurt and Robin certainly was. That's quite a drop."

"Aw . . ." George said with a sneer.

Before Robin could speak Tom went on. "Look here," he

said, "we've been having a pleasant evening and you're welcome to join us if you can act decent. If you can't I'll be obliged if you'll move on."

"Oh," George returned airily, "I wasn't intending to stay. I just came out for a breath of air. What I was going to tell you was a nice little gossip tidbit. Well, good-night for the present." And George sauntered on down the street.

But the happy atmosphere had been broken. Everyone wondered what the new bit of gossip was and there were some outspoken conjectures which caused Tom as host and general monitor to say finally that they had all better keep their thoughts to themselves.

"Come on," he added cheerfully. "I've got an idea. We haven't taken a trolley ride as a group for ever so long. Why don't we go now? The moonlight's just right, and old Emory would take us even if it's past hours. What do you say?"

"Good idea," Sandy Low seconded, "then if our friend George comes back he'll find the steps empty."

There were delighted cries from the girls and in a few minutes the party was walking down to the corner where the trolley made a stop. Old Emory, as they called him, was supposed to own part of the trolley and acted as though he owned it all. He had a sensitive heart for young people, especially young lovers, so he peered out now over his steel-rimmed glasses and tried to look stern and failed.

"What you mean, comin' up to me at this hour? Don't you know we stop at ten-thirty sharp?"

"Oh, Mr. Emory," Alice pleaded. "The night is so beautiful and we all *so* want a ride. Just for once couldn't you break the rule?"

The old Irishman looked at her for a moment and then said, "Pile in, then, the lot of you, but don't be botherin' me again at a time like this."

"We won't! We won't," chorused the voices, and in a few minutes, seated in the long seats with the night air swishing past them, the young people were borne out of the town, past the big Adair home, and on between harvest fields and gentle meadows until the country, with the moon showering silver upon it, had gathered them to itself.

A fold of Alice's thin dress had blown across Robin's knee and under its cover he grasped her hand and held it firmly.

"Alice," he said in a low voice, "I must see you soon alone. Will you come for a drive with me tomorrow afternoon? We can find a quiet spot in the woods back of your grandfather's house where we can talk. Will you?"

"Yes, Robin," very low.

"About three, then? I'm off on Saturdays, you know."

"I'll be ready."

There were gay sporadic bursts of song from the long seats, but in the main the sounds were muted whispers which were meant for one ear only. Old Emory, standing tall, with his proud hand on the wheel like a captain of a ship, glanced back occasionally noting the pretty heads resting on strong shoulders, and smiled, well pleased. He made the ride as long as the track would permit, even once doubling up at a junction, and when at last he had to swing the trolley to a stop at the crossing where the group had come aboard, his voice was very gruff, which fooled nobody.

"Well, here ye are, an' let me tell you you'll never get me out on a caper like this again. Keepin' me at work till this hour. Get off now, the lot of ye, an' see you behave yourselves. I don't want your parents dingin' at me."

They dismounted with many thanks and much praise and laughter, leaving old Emory pleased with himself and them.

"Come on back to the steps," Tom urged, "and have a last swig of lemonade to end the evening."

They trooped willingly over the sidewalk until they were in sight of the steps, then as if they were one, stopped short. A dark form sat there and from the pale light from the hall, as well as the moon, they could see it was George. As they went slowly on, he stood up, one hand in his pocket.

"Well Adair, the more I thought of it the more I felt there was no use waiting longer to even our score. So let's have it out right now if Tom will let us use their garden. We can see well enough. I feel all the more like it since I heard the news I got straight tonight. The Miss Adairs have each changed their wills in this fellow's favor. What have you to say to that, Adair?"

"I have this to say," Robin spoke in a clear, decisive tone. "I knew absolutely nothing about their intention until they called me into the parlor one day to hear Squire Weir read the new documents. They were already signed and witnessed by him and Molly Hart. Of course I appreciate it but I felt then as I do now, uncomfortable and embarrassed."

"I'll bet you do," George said with an ugly laugh. "All right, let's get on with the business in hand, or are you afraid to fight?"

Robin was standing near George now, and his keen eyes

had been searching him carefully. All at once he called Tom.

"Will you come here?" he said. "If we fight we'll need an umpire." He spread out his two hands so that all could see. "Tom, will you have George open his hands the same way before we begin."

"Open up, George."

"This is ridiculous," George said angrily, the one hand still in his pocket. "What's he up to, anyway?"

"Spread your hands wide open, George, or there will be no fight. Hurry up about it."

Reluctantly George spread the one hand and drew the other from his pocket. As he opened it, something fell from it. Tom was quickest and picked it up at once. It was a small, hard, round object wrapped in a bit of cloth. Tom removed the cloth and let the object fall upon the pavement, where it made the sound of metal upon stone.

"It was just a joke!" George began in a loud voice. "I only meant to scare him a little. Well, my hands are as wide open as yours, Adair, if you're not afraid to go ahead."

Robin's voice was cold as ice. "I think you know now, I don't have to fight," he said.

There was a shocked silence which no one seemed willing to break. George stood, looking wildly around as though he could not realize the situation in which he found himself. Then, with the judgment of his peers all about him in the deadly quiet, he turned and walked up the street toward his own home. When he was at last out of hearing the voices came all at once.

"What in the world has struck George? He's always been a nice fellow. Now, he really acts desperate," Sandy said.

"But he is," Betsy cried, her eyes full of tears. "He *is* desperate and that's what makes him behave this way. Oh, I'm so ashamed!"

Tom stood close to her and patted her shoulder.

"Don't worry," he said. "He'll get over it, and what happened just now may jolt him back into his normal senses. Come on, let's have our lemonade anyway. We'll make it this time, Sis."

"There's still plenty in the crock," Alice said, "it just needs ice."

There was soon laughter again but any further discussion of George was dropped out of deference to Betsy. There was to be noted, however, a new and respectful attitude toward Robin. At last, reluctantly, they all rose and the boys drew together for their final harmony. Then tenderly it fell upon the quiet air:

Good night, ladies, sweet dreams ladies . . .
Good night, ladies, we'll have to leave you now.

The next day was pure autumn gold. There was still a delicious summer warmth within it, but there was also in the air the spice of the first chrysanthemums and the first burnt leaf; and the luminous haze abroad through which one stepped was like the atmosphere of another world. Alice felt all this with a vague, nervous pleasure, as she waited for Robin that afternoon. He came promptly and tied the horse to the stone upping block while he came in to greet Mrs. Newcombe. That lady, as always, received him with an almost effusive pleasure, quoted a few lines from her favorite Tennyson, which Alice thought highly inappropriate:

> . . . in looking at the happy autumn fields
> And thinking of the days that are no more . . .

then with a motherly bustle saw the young people off from the front door.

"And drive carefully, Robin. That horse looks high-spirited."

"Oh, I will, never fear."

The horse plunged forward and they were on their way.

"I thought if you were agreeable we would take a little drive around the lake and then end up at the woods back of your grandfather's."

"That will be lovely. Oh, Grandfather is very much pleased with you."

"Not nearly as much as I with him," Robin answered. "He's the wisest and most delightful old gentleman I ever met. I wait pretty eagerly for his visits. In fact yesterday we had the long talk which ordinarily I would have had with your father but I still have trouble approaching him. He . . . he doesn't like me, I'm afraid."

"I know," Alice sighed. "When he once makes up his mind nothing seems to change him. Now, of course, since he's heard about the wills, he's worse than ever. Robin," she added hesitantly, "is there anything you could do or say that would make that situation look better for you? All your friends know you had nothing to do with it. It's just the miserable gossip."

"I know," he said. "I feel like a cad even though I *had* nothing whatever to do with it. Your grandfather says, 'keep your chin up and let the winds blow,' so I'll try to do that. But I'm not happy about it. I'd like to have the good will of the town, especially now. But anyway, let's enjoy our time if we can."

They drove slowly around the lake, serenely still now, as no canoes happened to be abroad at this hour, stopped for a moment at the farthest end to see the first red on the sassafras bushes and the first yellow on the birches, then drove toward the country road at the other side of town and finally to the woods which Mr. Means owned and kept cleared of underbrush. Robin tethered the horse to the stake and rider fence, then took cushions from the back of the surrey.

"I thought we might find a comfortable tree to lean against," he said laughing, "and we can sit on these if you're sure you will be warm enough. Should I bring a blanket too?"

"Why, it's still like summer temperature," Alice exclaimed. "But yes, bring the blanket just for a talking point. Mother still thinks you're in danger of pneumonia if you sit on the ground, even in July!"

They walked on until they found a great oak, its spreading branches still green, and here Robin laid the cushions with the blanket near for look's sake and they sat down very, very close to each other. For a few moments nothing was said, but Alice, looking up, saw his eyes upon her with an expression in them that made her realize the conversation would not be casual, and the color rose in her cheeks.

"I know," he began, "that I am being . . . I suppose you would call it precipitous. I know I should wait at least six months and then lead up to it. But I warned you once I was not naturally cautious and somehow I have to tell you honestly, without more delay what is in my heart. I *love* you, Alice! Ever since that first day when I looked into your eyes as I got off the train. Oh, my darling, I love you! Is there a chance, a hope that you can return it and some day marry me?"

Alice felt his hand lying next to hers, trembling. She caught it in both her own. "I am the one who should wait. It seems almost unmaidenly to be sure of myself so soon. But Robin, I must be honest too. I do love you with all my heart. And some day . . ."

But the sentence was never ended for his arms held her close and their lips met with young ecstatic ardor under the green boughs.

When the first raptures were over there was much of a serious nature to discuss. First there was Robin's quite natural desire to let the secret be known and to put a ring on his beloved's finger. Over against this was the certain opposition of Alice's father. It was finally decided that for the present they would tell only Mrs. Newcombe and Mr. Means, hoping that time would somehow work on their side in softening Mr. Newcombe's hard attitude.

"I would so like to tell the cousins of our engagement," Robin said regretfully. "I've grown so fond of them and I know this is going to please them, but the trouble is even though they would *try* to keep our secret, when their guests come to tea they would be sure to let a hint slip and then all would be out."

"And Squire Weir, too. They would likely drop some remark which he would take up and Grandfather says whatever the squire knows today the whole town will know tomorrow."

"Yes. I don't entirely trust that man, somehow. Don't ever breathe a word of this, Alice, but I don't think he liked that business of the wills. You see now he stands to lose quite a bit eventually and it's only human of him to resent it. Oh, I wish that whole idea had never entered their heads, bless them. So kind a thought it was but so sure to make trouble for me, somehow. However, don't let's becloud our happiness today. It's too wonderful to believe that you really love me. Let's just think about that, for our time's short enough."

"If it only weren't for George," Alice said. "I know all our friends will be happy for us. I'm so puzzled about him. He seems to have changed completely."

"He's gone off his chump, all right," Robin said, "but I'm sure I know why. He's wild because he's lost his girl. If I had lost you I'd feel the very same way. I hope I wouldn't show it as he's doing but I'd be beside myself just the same. The way I have George figured out is that he felt so sure of you he was just biding his time and then I suddenly appeared on the scene and upset all his plans. I'm sorry for him, really."

Alice took his hand in her own. "You're so kind, to feel this way after what happened last night. I'm still afraid he will hurt you."

Robin shook his head. "I don't think so, not physically, now. But I have a feeling he will take his venom out in gossip and I don't like that, I can tell you."

When it was almost time to go, Robin spoke hesitantly after a long kiss.

"I have a confession I would like to make, Alice. Oh, it's nothing bad," he said, smiling at the startled look on her face. "It is probably just silly but I don't want to have any secrets from you. It's about an ambition I've had since I was very young. I would like to *write*."

"To *write*," Alice echoed, amazed.

"Yes. I know it seems foolish. So many young people have this desire and it never comes to anything. And probably mine won't either. But at least I've had a few little verses published in papers back home and I've shown what I've done to your grandfather . . ."

"Oh, Robin, I'm so glad of that. What did he say?"

Robin flushed and swallowed in embarrassment. "Well, he was really very kind. He thinks I might have a little spot of talent, but that remains to be seen. He lent me some books, though, and of course I'll keep on trying. But please don't think too much about it. I only told you because I like to feel you know everything about me."

Alice was breathless. "But I think it's wonderful! I'm so proud of you. Will you some day write a book?"

"Oh, that's going too fast. I'll have to serve a long apprenticeship first. Your grandfather suggests sending some verses to the papers here and maybe later some little articles or sketches. All very small stuff but practice and fun to try. Alice, you won't tell anyone, will you?"

"Never," she said. "It will be another secret between us."

Robin made the horse trot very slowly as they drove back, holding it often to a walk. The afternoon with its soft haze was gathering all its gold into a sunset of blazing color. They watched it with eyes filled with wonder at its beauty and their own love.

"I never dreamed I could be so happy," Robin said, as they neared the town.

"Nor I," Alice told him with a tenderness she did not now have to conceal.

"When may I see you again?" he asked. "The times between are like deserts to me. Is any other party coming up soon?"

"Just the corn roast a week from tonight."

"What's that?" Robin asked quickly.

"Oh, I forgot you don't know about corn as we do. We always choose a nice orchard at one of the farms for the party — this time it's to be at the Stevens' — then the girls take sandwiches and cake and the boys bring the corn, roasting ears, we call them, but they really are boiled in a great kettle. Then we eat them with mountains of butter, and they are perfectly delicious and it's all great fun. If you ask Miss Jenny and Miss Kitty they will tell you all about it, for it's an old custom here. Would you care to escort me, sir?" she asked demurely.

He gave her a convulsive little hug. "There's only one trouble. It's a whole week away. I've got to see you in between."

"Betsy told me this morning that she has decided to take the bull (meaning George) by the horns and go on as usual. Just as though nothing had happened. She thinks that may be the best way to bring him to his senses. So she's going to have a steps party on Saturday night. Will you come?"

"I don't see why I shouldn't."

"I'm sort of afraid for you and yet I'm proud of you and everything may be perfectly normal."

"I think," Robin said hesitantly, "that from something your grandfather told me he's planning to have us both there to dinner on Sunday."

"Oh, *wonderful!* Shall we tell him then?"

"If I can keep it until Sunday."

Alice laughed. "I know. I doubt if I can hold out with Mother that long either. In any case going to Grandfather's will be like a real little celebration, won't it?"

"Yes, but considering Hepsy's interest in all that goes on I think it will be safer to tell Mr. Means before, don't you?"

"Of course. I forgot Hepsy. She would tell Molly Hart who would tell the Miss Adairs and then in no time the whole town would know." Alice looked worried. "It's just Father we have to be careful about. I don't want to estrange him. You understand, don't you, Robin?"

"Certainly I do. If I just knew how I could make him approve of me!"

"You might drop in Sunday night, sort of casually for a

little music. Father likes that. I'll tell you his favorites be-forehand. If he and Mother were both present he couldn't take exception to that."

They had reached the street and were drawing up before the Newcombe house when Mr. Newcombe appeared on the sidewalk before them. Robin smiled and spoke as he handed Alice out of the surrey and was about to shake hands before getting back into the driver's seat, when he was stopped.

"Just a minute, young man," Mr. Newcombe said. "Just where have you been with my daughter?"

"We took a drive, sir, to Hallett's Woods."

"You've been *in the woods?*"

"Why, yes sir, we have."

"Alice?"

"Yes, Father. It was beautiful there."

"No doubt. Now, young man, what did you do in the woods?"

"We talked."

"Was that all?"

Robin was silent, his face grim.

"Were there caresses exchanged there? Answer me."

Robin's strong chin was high. "Yes," he said, "there were. I kissed your daughter, Mr. Newcombe, but not until after I had declared myself in love with her."

"So, we get at the facts now. Well, young man, I have this to say. I, among others in this town, am not satisfied with the way you suddenly appeared here and took over the Adair sisters as you have done. I do not wish you to come to this house any more. I can't prevent you from seeing Alice when you're with the other young people but I *can* prohibit any more clandestine meetings *in the woods.*"

"Father," Alice burst out through her tears, "you are insulting us both."

"No, I'm just thinking of your good and stating my wishes. So, I will bid you good afternoon, Mr. Adair, and hope you will remember what I've just said."

Robin bowed deeply and said nothing. Alice came close to him as her father entered the door.

"I'm so embarrassed and so angry I don't know what to do. I hope you will forgive him. He's very old-fashioned. But how can we ever see each other . . . alone?" she ended as her eyes filled up.

Robin's face was flushed but he managed a smile. "I think we'll find ways. Above all, don't worry. I can't stand it to see you cry. I would dry your tears if I thought your father wouldn't suddenly come out and see me."

"But for him to think there was something wrong about our being *in the woods,* when they were so beautiful!"

" 'There's nothing either good or bad but thinking makes it so,' Shakespeare said, so let's just stick to him. And now, darling, don't worry, and good-bye. I only wish I dared say it properly."

He gathered up the reins and in a moment, with a last wave of his hand, drove off down the street. Alice went slowly into the house and to her own room. When Sally Ann rang the chimes as usual at six o'clock only three came to the table.

"I don't know what's keeping Alice," Mrs. Newcombe said anxiously. "I called but she didn't answer. Maybe she and Robin had a little tiff. I'll go and see."

Mr. Newcombe carefully watched his plate, while Tom watched him as his mother made her hasty exit. When she reached Alice's room, however, she was alarmed. The girl was not only weeping, she was sobbing.

"What in the world!" she exclaimed. "What happened? Oh, Alice, please tell me everything. Did you and Robin quarrel?"

"No! *No!*" the girl burst out. "Anything but that. Mother, he loves me and I love him, but when we came back to the house Father was there and he insulted us and told Robin he couldn't come here again and what will I *do?*"

Mrs. Newcombe's lips were grim. She half spoke as though to herself. "If it hadn't been for you and Tom over the years I would almost have . . ." She stopped suddenly as though frightened at the words which had almost come. "What I mean," she said distinctly, "is that you and Tom have always been such a comfort to me when your father was very *set* about something. Now, Alice, just dry your tears and pretend nothing has happened. This will take patience but it's sure to work out. You can count on me and certainly on your grandfather . . ."

"And the Miss Adairs."

"Oh, definitely, and that ought to be enough. Oh, my dear, just be happy in your love. I'm sure Robin is worth it. Come on now, down to dinner."

For several days Mr. Newcombe suffered acutely from the

fact that he had no opposition against which he could rail. No one spoke of his ultimatum; no one mentioned Robin at all. Alice was quiet but respectful, Tom unusually chatty about general affairs, Mrs. Newcombe, aside from frequent quotations from Tennyson, seemed her usual housewifely self. Mr. Newcombe, indeed, found himself all armed for a struggle which did not take place. As a result of this he was irritable and inclined to criticize everybody and everything. Even with this his family remained calm.

But Robin's attitude during this time was far from calm. He chafed, he raged within himself, he started to tell the cousins all, and then, before their serene countenances, checked himself. To their arch comments about Alice, however, he allowed his voice and manner to suggest his feelings, which seemed to send them into romantic little tremors. Every once in a while they threw into the conversation somewhat at random such remarks as, "This house is really large enough for *two* families." Robin never made a comment to this, though he gave them a knowing smile.

But while he did not unbare his soul to the cousins he did do so to Mr. Means, the first time the latter strolled into the office. When the story was told, the old gentleman swore steadily, good, round, old-fashioned oaths directed toward his son-in-law. Robin listened, fascinated. When there was a pause he drew a long breath and said, "Thanks. That's done me no end of good. I couldn't do it myself but I wanted to. Only now, what can I do about Alice? I've got to see her alone sometimes."

"Naturally. Well, let's see. Bill Newcombe wouldn't trust

his own grandmother so we've got to circumvent him somehow. Why couldn't Alice come up to see me Saturday afternoons when it's Hepsy's day off. You could happen in and we could all visit for a little until I would be seized with a sudden fit of drowsiness and retire to my room for a nap. The downstairs and porch then could be all yours? How does that strike you?"

"That would be heaven," the young man said. "How can I thank you?"

"By showing me some more of your 'stuff' as you call it."

Robin drew out some papers hesitantly from the under drawer of the desk. "Some of these verses are rather . . . well . . ."

"Mushy," David Means ended with a grin. "Well, they ought to be at your age and with a girl like Alice."

He read slowly, then read them through again and singled one out.

"Robin," he said, "this is good. If I thought your hat would still fit you I'd tell you to my mind it's *very* good. I believe it's publishable. Send it to a good magazine and try it out. I'll give you an address. This little animal fable is good in its own way, too. You could try it on *The Youth's Companion*. Have you done any more prose?"

"Just a bit of description of the town," Robin said, handing it over.

Mr. Means read the pages and then threw back his head and laughed. "It's uncanny," he said. "You've trapped us here in Callaway! Yes, this is the way the town must seem to a stranger! But," he added, "you've caught the beauty of the old place too. You've been accurate but kind. I don't think, my boy, you'll be bookkeeping all your life, but just now it's read, write, read, write in all your spare time. That gets results. *Never a day without a line,* is the old motto. At least that's what was given to me."

At Robin's quick question David nodded. "Oh, yes, I had the same desire when I was your age but the trouble was I didn't have the *divine spark,* and I believe you do. So, good luck, and let's talk business now."

But before the great account book was more than opened there was the sound of running feet outside the door, a sharp knock and then the figure of Charles at the entrance.

"Come quick," he said. "It's Miss Jenny. She tripped over the carpet on the step outside her bedroom and no one knows how it could have been loose an' she fell an' hit her head an' they've got her laid out on the bed an' I come straight for you, Mr. Robin, an' should I ought to get the doctor?"

"As fast as you can," Robin said. "Did you drive in?"

"No, I rode the mare. Miss Kitty's havin' hysterics an' Molly's carryin' on an' she says . . ."

"Get on," Mr. Means said sharply, "as fast as you can. Tell the doctor it's an emergency and to come out at once. I have my buggy. I'll drive Mr. Adair. Now *hurry!*"

"That will get rid of him, but I'll call Doc from here to make sure."

When the two men were seated in the buggy with Mr. Means applying the whip to the startled horse, Robin spoke with a lump in his throat. "Oh, I *hope* she isn't badly hurt. I didn't know how much I cared for her until I thought of her in real danger. I've grown terribly fond of them both."

"Robin," Mr. Means asked sternly, "did you know anything about that loose carpet?"

Robin turned toward him in amazement. *"Me?"* he said. *"Me?* Why, what could I know about that? Why did you ask me?"

And then Mr. Means gave a short laugh. "Because I like to hear your voice when it's surprised and indignant. That was *my* only reason. But if you recall your article on Callaway and its citizens you will remember that you mentioned that their experiences were somewhat limited and many of them therefore were inclined to make much out of even the smallest uncommon happening."

Robin looked thoughtful. "Yes, of course I've noticed that and this will be . . . will be . . ." He paused a moment. "By Jove," he went on. "Why you don't think . . . I mean no one could . . . could possibly . . . Oh, Mr. Means, you've terrified me by the very idea of any gossip about me. Damn those wills anyway."

"Amen to that. But now, just keep your shirt on, my boy. I didn't want to alarm you but forewarned is forearmed, you know. What probably happened was that Molly Hart forgot to put some tacks in when she was house-cleaning. I'll get her to mention this to Squire Weir and the town should know at once."

"I hope so," Robin said, his young voice troubled. "I certainly hope so."

## CHAPTER FOUR

MISS JENNY lay very quiet for several hours, too quiet, indeed, and then suddenly opened her eyes upon the doctor, Miss Kitty, Mr. Means, Robin and Molly Hart and said quite distinctly, "I really think for a moment I lost my footing. Most unusual for me, and *very* undignified. I hope nobody saw me. Molly, did you finish making the jelly?"

From that point on she was her normal self and the others made what excuses they might for their watchful attendance. "A very slight concussion," the doctor told Mr. Means and Robin in the hall. "As far as I can judge she's absolutely all right now, but it could have been serious. It *might* have been fatal. Let's have a look at that carpet."

There were three steps leading down from the sisters' bedroom wing at the rear of the house into the upper hall, all neatly carpeted. The top one, however, had not been firmly tacked, and still gaped open where Miss Jenny's heel had caught in it.

"Call me if you need me," the doctor said, "and get Molly to fasten that strip down good and tight."

"I'll have a talk with her right now," David Means said, as Robin went back to entertain Miss Jenny.

But Molly had been difficult. "I *did* tack it down," she said. "Haven't I been doin' that for twenty years? Somebody must have loosed it." And curiously, her face flamed as she said it.

David stayed to dinner partly to check on Miss Jenny and partly to be there if the squire came out. He did, his long, thin nose pointing, and his eyes very sharp behind his spectacles.

"Well, well, well," he sputtered. "My dear Miss Jenny, I just heard of the . . . the accident and I came at once. Should you be out of bed?"

"Why should I be in bed?" Miss Jenny said with some spirit. "I feel perfectly well except for the embarrassment of falling over my feet. I'd rather that was not talked about, Squire."

"Of course. Of course. But you must admit the circumstances . . ."

"Were very normal," Mr. Means finished calmly. "It's not the first time a lady's high heel has caught in a bit of carpet. Now, mind you, I don't hold with the writer of Ecclesiastes in everything he said, but I have an idea he had a pretty wide knowledge of women and when he kept harping on *vanity* . . ." He turned to smile at his old friend. "When a woman has as pretty a foot as Miss Jenny here, it's only natural for her to wear pretty shoes with fancy buttons and *high heels*. So, there you are!"

The squire looked nonplussed, Miss Jenny, flattered, and

Robin coughed suddenly into his napkin. Miss Kitty assumed a virtuous air. "I've told her often about that. Now I get all *my* shoes from Laird's here in town. They call them the *Stylish Common Sense,* and they are plenty good enough for women our age, but Jenny will insist on these French heels which I keep telling her are not safe."

"And so," said Mr. Means, "how is the great business world going, Squire? Stationery, et cetera?"

The squire was at a loss but tried to recover. "Fair. Fair," he said. "Usual trade. Some wedding invitations and such. But no one gets rich on stationery. Newspapers bring in the most. But I'll tell you one thing that shook us all yesterday afternoon. The Old Girl was ten minutes late! First time in anyone's memory. I tell you I felt queer."

"Any reason?" Mr. Means asked.

"Not a word. Conductor was mum, and the engineer and the brakeman were sort of nasty. Makes you wonder what's wrong with the world anyway with upsets like that, for the Old Girl has been as dependable as the sun itself. Could set your watch by her."

"Oh," Mr. Means remarked cheerfully, "there was probably a good reason and the world just may hold together a little longer. Are you able to listen to a little music, Jenny, if Kitty will play Robin's accompaniments again?"

They made it a short concert but Robin put his best into it, ending of course with "I'll Come to You, My Lad." Miss Jenny was ushered off to bed by Miss Kitty and Molly. Mr. Means had an earnest talk with Robin, leaving him phone instructions and certain directions and then he bore the

squire off, the latter still apparently in a state of repressed in-
dignation. Even on the way home Mr. Means kept up a
steady stream of casual conversation so that the squire's attempts at developing a mystery were in vain.

But subtly like a miasmic fog a question moved through
the town. The squire of course was burning to ask it of
someone, and when George Hastings stopped for the evening
paper he found an eager, listening ear. From that point on,
it became the question without an answer. Only the facts
were whispered hesitantly, Molly Hart was known to say
that the carpet had been securely fastened and that *someone*
must have loosed the tacks! Miss Jenny had fallen, narrowly
escaping serious, perhaps fatal injury. Who stood to gain if
the latter had been the case? There the whisperings paused.
No one would speak the name. That is, no one except
George Hastings, who seemed to relish the sound of it.

There was much undercover discussion, pro and con, with
the women, led by Mrs. Newcombe, but the majority of
them recounted the time they had been interrupted while
tacking down a carpet and the same thing could have happened to Molly Hart. Besides, one called upon another to
witness, that the heavy hall carpet, also on the steps, had been
down for years for Miss Kitty wouldn't give it up because of
the rose pattern. So there just *could* have been a small hole
in it after it was beaten on the clothesline the day before.
The young people, unconscious arbiters of opinion, took the
matter lightly, first because they all liked Robin and second,
because they felt George Hastings had shown a mean and
suspicious spirit about the whole thing. So, as days passed

there was a gradual lessening of both meaningful glances and conversation while the town apparently settled into its even tenor. This was especially noticeable after Miss Jenny, Miss Kitty, and Molly Hart, with Robin escorting them, had appeared in church each Sunday and occupied their usual forward pew with due ceremony. To the many inquiries as to her health, Miss Jenny said with emphasis, "I'm very *well,* thank you," implying that the subject of the fall was closed.

Only the squire in his stationery store, George Hastings at the carpet factory and Mr. Newcombe at the bank kept alive the bit of dim, dark fog which had at first spread subtly through the town.

"I don't like the look of things," Mr. Newcombe remarked to his wife in the privacy of their bed-chamber. "I mean Jenny's accident."

"Oh, Bill, don't keep harping on that. Anybody is likely to have a fall. And remember, Jenny must be in her late seventies if she's a day."

"But there was a *reason* for this," he persisted.

"There's a reason for everything, but it doesn't have to be a suspicious one," Mrs. Newcombe countered. "Robin is a nice young man and the more I think of it, the more ridiculous it seems that he would ever plan anything to hurt Miss Jenny. He looks you straight in the eye, for one thing, which is more than some people do."

This parting shot struck home, for with all Mr. Newcombe's jocularity with his cronies and with other bankers and his friendly shrewdness with new customers, he always looked a bit to the side of their faces or just over their heads during conversation. That his own wife had noted this and made it a basis of comparison left within him a feeling of bitterness immediately transferred to young Adair.

Meanwhile Alice and Robin, treading delicately, as it were, among their plans, had managed some hours of delight together at her grandfather's when Robin was free and Hepsy away. While Alice knew that as a rule Mr. Means read until the dinner hour, his sudden attacks of drowsiness now were so well simulated that no stranger could have questioned them. When he had gone to his room the lovers, looking deep in each other's eyes had confided their hearts' utter trust.

"Oh, Alice, you know . . ."

"How could I imagine such an unspeakable thing. Let's just go on to talk of something else." So they did, hands clasped. They spoke shyly and tenderly of the arrangements they would one day make for their life together; they spoke of Robin's writing and once he brought a little poem for her to read. It was the one Mr. Means had thought was the best, so he had copied it with care and written *To Alice* at the top. She read it, wept a little over it and said she would put it in an envelope and sleep with it under her pillow.

"If I could only tell you my love for you in as beautiful a way," she said wistfully.

"But you *have*," he said, taking her into his arms. "Just by being you."

Their hours together brought out mutual interests of which they had been unaware. From Mr. Means's shelves they borrowed the poets which they found they both knew best. Then close on the old porch swing they sat reading the words of the great lovers before them, each wondering how the old lines could possibly express so much of their own feeling. Sometimes they paused in sheer astonishment at their reactions.

"I never thought any girl would understand . . ."

"I never dreamed I would find a man who would know . . ."

The steps party at Betsy's had come off without incident. Alice had been firmly of the opinion that Robin should go and act as though nothing had happened. Although George had asked pointedly, "And how is Miss Jenny feeling, Robin?" he had answered calmly, "Why, unusually well, I think," and no other reference had been made by anyone.

There had not been as much gayety nor as much singing as at the former party, but enough to give satisfaction to the guests; there was, indeed, a general air of friendliness toward Robin, for with the uncanny perception of youth the young folks seemed to sense and approve of the love between him and Alice, though no word of this would be spoken for some time to come. It all raised Robin's spirit, however, and he joined in the fun and the quiet jokes with the rest of them.

When it was time to leave, Tom said his good-byes to Betsy in the hall and then (as they had prearranged) walked slowly down the street behind Alice and Robin ready to join them if Mr. Newcombe suddenly appeared.

"Everyone is awfully kind," Robin said, adding, "I don't know anyone I'd like as much for a brother-in-law some day as Tom."

Alice squeezed his hand. "I like to hear you say that. I'm so fond of Tom myself and then the other part of what you said makes everything seem so real as though . . . as though it's actually going to happen one day."

"Can you doubt it," Robin said, "after all our planning, and all our love? But when can I see you again, since you say your father is getting suspicious about your visits to your grandfather?"

"Yes. We'll have to watch out for that. But the corn roast will be coming soon. The boys put it off so we'd have another full moon and they thought the corn would be better too. I know you'll enjoy this for it's something you never would have in England."

"Never," Robin smiled.

"You see the boys bring big horse blankets to spread under the trees and we girls all take cushions, so it's really quite cozy and rather like a picnic."

"Except that the corn is the pièce de résistance."

"Exactly."

"I hope the moonlight won't be too bright," Robin said, looking down at her. "Just now your nice brother is looking the other way." He kissed her in the shadow of the vine-covered brick house where all was quiet and the elder New-combes, secure in the thought of Tom's chaperonage, had gone to bed.

But strange currents were running like small turbulent underground streams through Callaway, affecting widely diverse persons. There was Squire Weir, still smiling unctu-ously behind his stationery counter, still making what excuses he could to go out often to see the Miss Adairs, but all the time feeling a rankling bitterness that what would have been for him a very pleasant bequest, indeed, if he lived longer than either, had been snatched away from him by this young interloper, this Robin, whose place in the household of the ladies was still, in his mind, open to question. In this opinion he was strongly supported by Mr. Newcombe and they had many low-voiced talks together on the subject in the evenings on quiet street corners.

There was also, of course, George Hastings, who, feeling himself under a cloud among his fellows, was more and more convinced that the cloud surrounding Robin Adair had grown steadily darker. In fairness to poor George it must be said his heart was torn and sad and each time he saw Alice's face alight with the sweetness of love he cursed himself for being a slow, stupid, stubborn fool. But this attitude of mind only increased his rancor toward Robin.

Then there was poor Molly Hart, going about her appointed tasks with a new and terrible discovery. In her previous humdrum life, cooking and cleaning and waiting upon her ladies, her innocent and unperceptive mind had been quite unaware that such a thing as *love,* a burning, passionate, demanding love, existed. Now, not only her mind but her heart knew also. She woke with red, sleepless eyes in the mornings; her lips trembled as she passed the serving dishes to Robin at dinner or listened to his encomiums when she made his favorite popovers for lunch. So little she could do for him. So little she could say to him. So infinitely far he was above her but oh, how great was her love! She never confided the real secret to Hepsy, although it was always a relief to walk with her as usual, and once conversation had gone like this: "Mr. Robin certainly relished his vittles tonight." And, a few minutes later, "Mr. Robin asked me to wait in the hall and listen to the music for he'd heard me singin' that 'Whistle an' I'll Come to You, My Love.'"

"They're all singin' that," said Hepsy. "For my part I think he's clear gone on Miss Alice. You ought to see him look at her when they're at our house for dinner!"

"I feel sort of tired all at once. I think I'll be gettin' on home," Molly said abruptly.

"Why what's got into you? We ain't hardly started," said Hepsy.

But Molly spoke no more and went back.

There were, of course, other underground currents like small spring freshets but they seemed to flow briefly and then dry up. There was always also on the surface the spoken words of gossip which served to stimulate conversation where ladies gathered to have tea or sat in small groups at church sociables. But these, too, drifted a moment and were gone. Miss Jenny had never looked better in her life, one called upon another to witness, nor had Miss Kitty; Robin Adair was a handsome young man and always pleasant as a basket of chips, now wasn't he? And oh, didn't it look as though he and Alice Newcombe were really getting serious? Hush, here come Mrs. Newcombe. They say she's quite agreeable but that he is *terribly* opposed especially since . . . you know what.

So the stronger currents and the tiny freshets and the fleeting words all blent together in Callaway's early autumn days, while the town itself with its many vine-covered brick houses or verandahed frame ones, its quiet, shady streets, the important business structures of the carpet factory, the hardware store and the First National Bank all stood solidly in their places. Young people suddenly fell in love; older people suddenly began to take trolley rides instead of long walks and the Old Girl was once again late, this time by four minutes, causing Squire Weir to inquire darkly of his neighbor, "What's the world coming to? It's changing all right. Yes sir, we've lived to see changes."

The corn roast was an institution. After the normal pleasures possible during the hot summer and before the first real snow came to bring out the spanking cutters and the pure music of the sleigh bells, there came this hiatus in time, this climatic benison which brought its own special diversion impossible to any other season. But as Alice baked her famous devil's food cake that morning and made her quota of sandwiches, she nursed a grievance in her heart, and sadly enough it was against her father. She hated the deceit, the subterfuge, all the evasions now necessary if she and Robin were to meet. It took away something precious and openly warm with delight which the season and their love should have brought. It also meant that even with all their planning they could see each other much less often.

"Well," she thought to herself as she iced the cake, "thank heaven for the corn roast!"

At dinner Mr. Newcombe looked at his daughter. "How are you going to this shebang tonight?"

"With Tom and Betsy."

"Well, that's good. What about George?"

"I don't know anything about him."

"Now, I want to say again to you that George is a fine . . ."

"Upstanding young man," Tom went on. "We know his family. We know his prospects. We know he's considered himself a suitor for a year or more."

Mr. Newcombe looked sharply at his son, but that young man's face was completely sober and without apparent guile. His father said, "Well, you took the very words out of my mouth, Tom. I'm glad you feel as I do. George is probably offended now and no wonder, but he'll get over it. Have a good time tonight. This Adair fellow I assume is not going."

Alice choked slightly but Tom answered. "You can't tell who will turn up at a corn roast, but rest assured I'll keep my eyes open."

"Good," said Mr. Newcombe.

Since the nights were growing a bit cool Alice wore a thin, blue, wool dress with a little jacket to match which her mother had made for her. She tried hard not to admit to herself how pretty she looked. Her mother spoke to her often of the dangers of vanity. "Fight it, Alice. You know it's the last thing that dies in a woman. So watch it."

"Oh, I will," Alice always returned, and just now after removing the shine from her nose with a bit of chamois and settling two more hairpins in her pompadour, she hurried down the stairs, praying hard for humility.

It was Tom who upset her petitions as she stood ready to

get into the surrey. "Whew!" he said. "If Robin and George both see you tonight in that outfit there will be a battle royal. I may add that I'll bet on Robin any time."

"Oh Tom, you don't think they'll fight again, do you?"

"No, I don't. I think George really got his comeuppance the last time. But there's still no love lost between them, that's sure, and George has a mean streak in him I never suspected."

"It certainly doesn't run in the family!"

"You bet it doesn't," Tom answered with emphasis. "Betsy's all cut up over the way things have been going."

Betsy herself was dimpled and smiling as she got into the front surrey seat beside Tom, who looked at her as though he was happy that he need fear no rival.

Robin had planned to join them at the turn of the road beyond the Adair house, and there he was now waiting apparently with eagerness. He got into the back seat, his eyes speaking their admiration, and settled himself as close to Alice as possible.

"What a night!" he said, after speaking to the others, for the full moon was just edging above the horizon.

"Made to order," Tom echoed. "By the way, should we give him some directions about eating roasting ears out of doors? Hard enough to do it politely at the table, but out in the open we just sort of let 'er rip, as it were. The application of lots of butter to a hot ear of corn doesn't exactly make for . . ."

"Delicacy," Alice laughed. "But we girls take loads of napkins and tea towels and anyone can use them for *bibs* or mop themselves up afterwards, whichever they choose. Oh, Robin, I think you're going to like this party."

"I rather think I am," he said, drawing Alice a shade closer.

They drove on through the countryside, softened by dusk, past the mill through a woods, coming out at last at the spreading white farmhouse of the Stevenses and the orchard at the side of it. Already they could see a good fire burning with the great iron kettle above it. There was a medley of voices under the apple trees, much running to and fro and then shouts of welcome for the newcomers as the horse was tied and the occupants of the surrey joined the others. Alice showed Robin around with a pretty little air of possessiveness and introduced him to some of the country people he had not met before.

"Now come and see where the real work is going on," Tom called.

A half dozen boys were seated on a blanket with a huge pile of corn ears beside them. These they were stripping of their husks, handing the tender bare ears to the boys who laid them on piles on a table next to the large iron pot of water. On other tables, which had been brought apparently from kitchen or woodshed, were great prints of butter, sandwiches, and cakes at the farthest end for dessert.

"Everybody here now?" Bill Stevens called. "Can we start putting in the corn?"

The girls meanwhile had been getting old kitchen plates, knives and napkins from their baskets and when everyone was supplied they gathered as near as they could to the boiling kettle into which the Stevens boys were dropping the corn.

"Don't overcook it now. Mother says five minutes is enough," Bill kept saying to his brother.

"Here you are, Robin," Tom called soon, as he lifted two ears with long pincers from the kettle and put them on Robin's plate. "Watch out! They're hot. But by jumpin' jiminy, you'll find they're good."

The water bubbled, the corn grew quickly tender, and soon everyone, seated or standing, was spreading butter lavishly over the golden kernels.

"I never tasted anything like this in my life," Robin kept repeating.

"And you're growing adept at it too," Tom said, mopping a rill of butter from his own face. "Will we ever want anything else, girls, after this?"

"More corn! More corn!" the boys chorused.

But at last even the mound of sandwiches was attacked and everyone sat down, replete and relaxed on the blankets and cushions to savor slowly the ham and chicken delicacies made in Callaway's most capable kitchens.

"This is fun!" Robin kept saying to Alice, his face boyishly happy. "This is the best fun I ever had in my life. I've missed an awful lot, I realize, but I'm making it all up now. In many ways," he added, his face close to hers.

It was when the girls were starting to cut the cakes that the quick beat of a horse's hooves were heard on the country road. Everyone stopped to listen and then saw Charles, the Adair sisters' man-of-all-work, ride straight through the gap in the fence and come up to the young people now gathered anxiously to greet him.

"It's Miss Kitty," he began. "They sent me post off to get you, Mr. Robin. She's awful sick. They've got the doctor but he's plain baffled. He says if it was anyone but Miss Kitty he'd swear she'd been pizened."

"*Poisoned,*" the word went with horror from lip to lip.

"You're to come right off, Mr. Robin. She's askin' for you. You can ride behind me on the mare."

"I'll drive him in," Tom said promptly. "We'll get there just about as fast."

"Should I . . ." Alice asked.

"No," said Tom. "You just wait here and I'll come back for you girls. Come on, Robin. It's probably just a silly scare. Well, have a good time till we get back," he called as he and Robin ran toward the surrey.

In a few minutes the sounds of the rider and the driver grew fainter and finally disappeared into silence. Alice's face was white as she cut the devil's food cake and Betsy's hand trembled on her own knife. The other girls were gathered close, discussing the shocking news. "Oh Alice, you don't think . . ."

"Of course I don't think. What do you take me for?"

"But coming just after Miss Jenny's fall, there's bound to be . . . be *talk.*"

"Of course there will be. There's talk in this town no matter what happens."

"But what if . . . oh what if Miss Kitty should *die*. Poison's such a dreadful thing."

"She won't die," Alice said slowly. "And I just *know* it wasn't poison! Miss Jenny told me herself that they were having chicken and mashed potatoes and string beans and sassafras tea for dinner and what could be wrong with that, I ask you?"

"Alice, you're wonderful. You're so calm. If it was Tom that was under suspicion for anything I think I'd die. I sometimes wonder if you really care for Robin at all."

Alice raised her white tear-stained face and looked at her friend. "I wouldn't wonder if I were you. Let's get some more of the cakes cut. No one can talk too much while they are eating it."

Meanwhile, as the surrey rattled after the mare and its rider, Robin spoke his mind.

"I've never really talked about the various happenings to you, Tom, but now with this, I must. I love the old ladies. They've been unspeakably kind to me and I've grown very, very fond of them as I've told your grandfather. I hate the thought of these God-damned wills which of course I had nothing to do with. I'm terribly worried about Miss Kitty. If her trouble should really prove to be poison I would feel as though somebody — I don't know who — was trying to . . ."

"Pin something on you," Tom finished.

"I guess that expression would do as well as any. But you can see where it leaves me. I just hope you won't doubt me."

"Good Lord, no," Tom said with vehemence. "I think I can tell an honest man when I see him. We'll just hope for the best out here."

But the great stone house was lighted from top to bottom. The doctor's buggy was still in front as was also that of Squire Weir. Robin groaned and Tom muttered under his breath. Once in the great hall, Miss Jenny threw her arms about Robin.

"Oh, my dear boy, I'm so glad you've come! I've been so terribly worried over Sister Kitty. The doctor said right away she ought to go to the hospital but she won't do it so he brought a nurse and Squire Weir was here anyway which was such a comfort. Oh, Robin, the doctor says it might be poison. Where would she get that in *this* house. Oh, I'm shaking all over with the shock of it."

Robin put his strong young arms about her.

"Don't worry, Cousin Jenny. Is she even a little bit better?"

"Yes, the last half hour the doctor says the symptoms are not so alarming. She's quieter. She wants to see you, dear."

"I'll go right up. Come along. Just hold on to me, Cousin Jenny. Tom will wait for us."

They mounted the stairs to meet the squire in the upper hall. His nose was quite definitely longer than usual and his eyes more piercing behind their steel rims.

"Well," he said to Robin with a world of meaning in his tone. "So we have a *second* accident. What a very strange and alarming coincidence!"

Robin looked through him and did not reply, as they went on to Miss Kitty's room. She lay, a frail little sunken wisp of herself from her time of retching. She managed a smile for Robin, however, as he stooped to kiss her.

"I'm better," she said faintly, "now that you're here. Tell me about . . . the . . . corn roast."

So, very gently, his lips near to her ear and his eyes on the doctor for sanction, he told her all the details. She listened, smiled often and finally fell asleep, holding his hand fast. In the outer hall Robin spoke decidedly to the doctor.

"I want to hear all the details of this if you will be so kind. The word *poison* will be freely circulated, as you know."

"And rightly," put in the squire belligerently.

The doctor, although short, always gave the impression of height when he made any professional pronouncement.

"If you don't mind, Squire," he said now, "I would like to talk to young Mr. Adair alone for a few minutes."

The squire took Miss Jenny down the stairs with an affected gallantry while the nurse slipped into Miss Kitty's room.

"Now," said the doctor, "I realize what's on your mind and I'll tell you all I know. About an hour after dinner Jenny called me to say Kitty was very sick. I hurried out. She was almost in convulsions. I wanted to take her right to the hospital but she refused flatly, sick as she was. Maybe you've been here long enough to know that when one of the Adair girls makes up her mind, wild horses can't change it. I got equipment and a nurse from the hospital and we worked fast. She improved but it had to me all the earmarks of poison. At the moment she's quiet, the nurse will stay with her all night and knowing her resilience she will likely be bright as a bee in the morning. But I don't like the episode and I know you don't, for different reasons."

"You're quite right."

"I've questioned Molly Hart, who got the dinner. I can't get much out of her. She's a queer one. The only information that might help us was that she went to the woods yesterday afternoon to dig fresh sassafras roots. Now I happen to know that there are some questionable mushrooms growing near those sassafras bushes, but so does Molly. So does everybody else. Even children know to let them alone. Also Molly wasn't after mushrooms so I can't see any connection. Aside from that I can't dig up a single reason why poison should come into the picture at all. Of course my diagnosis may be wrong. The laboratory tests will show up the truth. But Adair, I know the spot you're in even without benefit of Squire Weir. That fellah should be married and have six kids and then he wouldn't be a gossipy old fuddy duddy."

Robin gave a short laugh but stopped suddenly, his face grave enough.

"I will answer any questions you may want to ask me, doctor."

The doctor looked him in the eye. "I'm an old friend of David Means," he said, "and when he vouches for a man I'll take his word any time. If this should prove to be a mild case of poison I think our business will be to keep our mouths shut and our eyes open."

Robin wrung the hand held out to him just as the nurse appeared at Miss Kitty's door.

"She wants you," she said to Robin.

"I think she'll sleep tonight but if she keeps asking for you . . ." the doctor said.

"I'll be right here. I won't go to bed."

"You really love the old ladies?"

"I do. They took me in and gave me a family when I had none. I would do anything for them."

"You were at a party?"

"Yes. A corn roast. My first one," he smiled.

"You don't mind missing the end of it?"

"Compared to helping Miss Kitty? Certainly not. How could you ask?"

"Good boy," the doctor said. "I'll check before I leave and keep my ear open tonight too."

When Robin leaned over Miss Kitty's bed she grasped his hand with a little sigh of content.

"I feel so much better when you're near," she said. "Could you look in on me once in a while during the night?"

"I'll be out here in the hall. You'll only have to speak to me or tell the nurse and I'll be right beside you. Do you feel better?"

"Oh, so much. I don't know whatever happened to me. The doctor and the nurse did a dreadful thing to me, really quite *unbecoming* to a lady, but it did help. Do you like sassafras tea?"

"I never tasted any. Was . . . was yours good tonight?"

"I guess so. I didn't really notice. I think, Robin, I'll take a little nap now. And you'll be near by?"

"Right in the hall. You have only to speak and I'll come."

"Dear, dear Robin," she said weakly and fell at once to sleep.

Robin smiled at the nurse, who was old enough to have a sympathetic heart and young enough to be stirred by Robin's good looks and charm. They arranged their duties for the night, then having earlier, after his first words with the doctor, hurried down to give Tom a chance to go back to the party with a few wise words for the crowd in general and a special good-night for Alice in particular, Robin glanced at the parlor, where the squire was still holding forth to Miss Jenny, and then went on to the kitchen to find Molly Hart, if he could. She was there, sitting at the table, her head bowed on her hands. He made his tone very casual.

"Hello, Molly!"

She looked up, startled with swimming eyes. "Mr. Robin, you know I never did nothin'. I just made them a good dinner an' . . ."

"Of course you did. But now I wish you would do something for me. I had plenty to eat at the corn roast, but somehow all this fright and anxiety about Miss Kitty has left me with the most awfully empty feeling. Could you fix me a sandwich and a cup of tea?"

Molly's response was all but electrical. She sprang from her chair. "Of course I could. Oh, Mr. Robin, it's the very first time you've sat out here with me an' asked me for a cup of tea or anything. I'll only be a minute. How's Miss Kitty?"

"Much better, the doctor thinks. She likes me to be near her and so I'm going to sit all night in the upper hall where I can get to her quickly if she calls."

Molly turned from making the sandwich, her cheeks aflame.

"Oh, Mr. Robin, my room's just next to Miss Kitty's down the hall and if you are setting there I just thought . . . you see you may get sleepy and if you'd want to come into my room and rest I would stay awake and listen and tell you if she calls. You'd be more comfortable, Mr. Robin, really you would."

"Thank you, Molly, but I think I'll just stay in the hall."

Molly came close. "If you'd want to come in it would be all right with me. I mean . . . I mean it would be . . ." the words seemed to slip out without her volition ". . . such a good chance . . ."

Her red face was suffused with tears of embarrassment that the dark secret of her heart was out. Robin looked carefully at the table before him.

"You're a nice girl, Molly, and you must always stay that way. I wonder if the tea is ready?"

"Just about. It only has to *mask* a bit longer. That's the word you use, ain't it?"

"I guess so. I never thought of it. Was the sassafras good tonight?"

Molly stiffened perceptively.

"I don't know. I didn't taste none."

"But I thought you liked it?"

"I just didn't feel for any tonight. I was too worried about Miss Kitty."

"Did Miss Jenny have some?"

"She never drinks it."

"Any left for me? I ought to try it for it's an American drink."

"No, there ain't. I washed out the teapot good, I'll tell you."

Robin looked up then. "Any reason for washing it so well tonight?"

"Yes, there was. It was on account of the squire. He's always snoopin' around but this time he was worse than usual. I just thought what he don't know won't hurt him so I washed everything up in a hurry an' put them away. I don't hold with the squire, Mr. Robin. An' here's your tea."

"Won't you have a cup with me? And what's wrong with the squire?"

Molly's face was suffused with her emotion. She seated herself gently on the kitchen chair as though a spell might be broken. "My, Mr. Robin, this is cozy, ain't it? Just the two of us havin' tea together. It's like sometimes I've dreamed about."

"A cup of tea is always cozy," Robin answered, "but what's this about Squire Weir?"

Molly leaned confidentially closer. "Well, I'll tell you. He's always makin' excuses to come out to the kitchen here when he comes to see the ladies. 'I must go an' have a word with Molly,' he says, like butter wouldn't melt in his mouth an' I can hear Miss Kitty sayin', 'Now isn't that sweet an' thoughtful of the squire,' she says. But they don't see him *goosin'* me every time I turn around an' many's the time I've been in his store he's tried to get me to go in behind the counter to see some new stationery an' I get out as fast as I can. Do you know what I think, Mr. Robin?"

"What?" he answered, glancing nervously over his shoulder.

"Well," Molly pronounced distinctly, "I think he's an old goat an' them's the worst kind."

"Dear me," said Robin guardedly, as though the expression was the only safe rejoinder.

"An' I'll tell you something about men, Mr. Robin. If I

was in a deep woods in the dead of night alone with you I'd never be afraid. I guess I'd just be . . . well, hopin' mebbe, though I oughtn't to say that right out like that. But if I was alone at night there with the squire I'd be scared to death. That I would."

"Mr. Adair," called the nurse's voice from the upper hall.

"I must go, Molly, but thank you so much for the tea. It was a good bracer."

Molly rose too and stood looking up into his face, the tears wet on her cheeks.

"You don't think the worse of me, Mr. Robin? I couldn't bear that."

"No, Molly, of course I don't, but I must hurry on now, to Miss Kitty."

She still stood as though by a kind of mesmerism the strength of her desire could restrain his leaving. He looked at her tear-stained, love-stricken homely face with its touching appeal and then, on the impulse, touched her forehead lightly with his lips and turned hurriedly toward the doorway. In it stood Squire Weir, apparently relishing the scene he had just witnessed.

Robin's throat felt dry. "I must go on up as fast as possible," he said at random.

"Yes, I should think so," the squire said. "Go on. I'll stay and have a word with Molly."

"No!" Robin was surprised at his own vehemence. He caught the older man's arm. "I want you to come along with me," and he propelled the squire along the passage. "I want to talk to you," he added.

"Oh, I don't think any explanation is necessary."

"But I do," said Robin. "You may have drawn a very wrong conclusion from what you just saw."

"Oh, I think not," responded the squire, with a peculiar grin.

"In any case I want to explain. Molly has paid me the very questionable favor of thinking she's in love with me. I've turned this aside of course, and spoken to her as sensibly as I could today, but was glad to have a cup of tea. After the nurse's call when I stood up to go she looked so forlorn and so pathetic, that as you saw I just touched her forehead with my lips. I probably shouldn't have done it, but I really pity the girl."

"Oh, 'pity is akin to love,'" the squire quoted with something like a sneer.

"It's nothing of the sort. In this case anyway. I've told you all there is to tell and I expect to explain to Cousin Jenny and Cousin Kitty just as I have to you. Well, here we are at Miss Kitty's room. Are you coming in?"

"I think I'll visit with Miss Jenny. The doctor may likely call back and I think I should be here. I don't like these odd coincidences, and just remember, young man, as far as I'm concerned you are *being watched*."

Robin looked him in the eye as nearly as possible. "Thank you, and I'll reciprocate," he said, as he went through the door leaving the squire staring after him.

Miss Kitty was weak but comfortable. She held out a thin hand and Robin grasped it warmly in his own.

"I think I've had another nap, but I'll sleep better if you stay near me tonight."

"I'll be right here in the hall, as soon as I get a dressing gown. Molly gave me a cup of tea in the kitchen," he added.

"Such a good girl, Molly. And so quiet. I don't believe she ever thinks of anything except her work."

"Perhaps not," Robin answered.

## CHAPTER FIVE

As THE DOCTOR had predicted, Miss Kitty, after a long night's sleep, sat up the next morning against her pillows, ate a light breakfast with relish and told the nurse tactfully that there was no further need of her. Miss Jenny intervened to say it was the doctor who had arranged for her coming and he must be consulted as to the length of her stay. Robin went into the room before he left for his office. He had dozed a little off and on through the night but had kept a careful watch and the morning light had found him heavy-eyed. However, several cups of Molly Hart's strong coffee had brought him wide awake. Miss Jenny at breakfast tried to engage Molly in conversation but she was stolidly silent.

"The nurse says Miss Kitty had a wonderful sleep, Molly. Isn't that good news?"

No answer.

"Mr. Robin sat all night outside Sister's door. Wasn't that kind of him?"

Molly turned abruptly and went back to the kitchen.

"You mustn't pay too much attention to Molly's moods, Robin. You can see she's still upset about Sister Kitty."

As Robin stood by the bed he was amazed at the change in its occupant. The little shrunken shell which had been Miss Kitty last night had now, after the relaxed comfort of her sleep, filled out again to her bright and normal self with color in her cheeks and her ready smile.

"I think it was knowing you were right out there that made me feel so safe," she told Robin. "And now you see I'm really quite well. Thank you, dear boy. What a blessed comfort you are to Sister and me!"

"Not as much as you both are to me," he replied. "I can't tell you how glad I am you are better."

As he was leaving the great front portico Robin met the doctor coming in. The latter's face was grave, in spite of Robin's good report.

"I pulled some strings and got the laboratory report early. It's not good. They found in the stomach contents some traces, slight but still there, of arsenic, of all things."

"Good God. What now?"

"I know Falk, the laboratory head. I've done my best to keep this quiet, but leaks are bound to occur. We've got to be prepared for them. Of course she had lost some of the meal before I got there with my equipment, which only makes it harder. I'm going to canvass the premises after I check Kitty this morning and try to find the source of the stuff. It's just possible Charles may have some in his little greenhouse. He's always mixing concoctions to kill potato bugs. But," he added, "even if I find some, we'll still be in the dark as to how it got into Kitty's food."

"Wouldn't she taste it?"

"No, that's the devil of it. It has no taste. That's why it's always popping up in mystery books. Well now, Robin, do a little pragmatic lying. If the word *arsenic* ever got bandied about, the town would jump over itself. So I am saying that it looks as though some bad mushrooms had sprung up too close to the sassafras roots and I want you to quote me. Just that and nothing more at the present. I have your promise?"

"You certainly have. I would do anything to make the situation better. I'd even go back to England."

"What good would that do?"

"Well, it's hard to explain but while I've done nothing wrong I've a miserable feeling that some one is trying to make it look as if I had, and if I could get out of the way . . . oh, I know I sound muddled."

But the doctor interrupted him sharply. "Will David Means be in your office today?"

"I imagine so."

"No one can hear you as you talk?"

"I'm sure not."

"Then shut the door and tell him the whole story. He's as safe as the tombs. But not to another soul."

Robin reached his hand. "You have my word," he said simply.

As he walked along the pavement to where he could catch the town-going trolley, Robin's heart was heavy. His eyes were still red, not only from lack of sleep but more from the new burden of unhappiness and alarm which lay upon him. Something ominous was abroad, something evil. It was touching — had indeed already touched — the old cousins, and no matter how he tried to put it aside he had the desperate fear that this threat hanging over them was related to him. He looked at it all objectively. As far as he knew he had only one real enemy, George Hastings, and in spite of his pugnacious actions these "accidents" as Squire Weir had called them were certainly not in his line. But the squire himself! Ah, there was a more likely wolf in sheep's clothing. And only tonight the mildness of the sheep had been dropped and the wolf fangs bared. It was puzzling, for even at the worst, if one of the sisters should die, the squire would still not come into any inheritance. But wait! Robin thought to himself. If it could so be arranged that to outward appearances Robin himself had been guilty of a crime or the attempt, then the squire's righteous wrath could be directed against him so that the will or wills could be changed to their original form. It would take a great deal to alter the cousins' affection for him, he knew, but if it came to something monstrous . . .

He drew a long, heavy sigh. Why must pain of the heart follow hard upon happiness? Why did unbearable burdens fall so soon upon bliss? He must get some word to Alice, perhaps through her grandfather or Tom. It would be hard to look into her clear eyes and tell her less than the truth, but he had given his word. As he entered the office, for the first time it looked drab and the books on the desk ponderous. The spirit seemed to have gone out of him. Even the creek, where he and Alice had spent so many happy hours in the canoe, seemed now but a dull little stream. He took off his coat and tried to settle down to work but his eyes kept turning to the front door. When David Means finally entered

Robin jumped up and clutched him as though he feared he might suddenly be spirited away.

"I can't tell you how glad I am to see you," he began. "I'm afraid I can't keep books today."

David looked at him keenly, the pale face, the reddened eyes, the unsteady hands.

"Well now," he said, pointing to one of the big leather chairs, "let's sit down and talk the thing over. Tom came in this morning with a cock and bull story about Kitty's being *poisoned*. Arsenic, I suppose."

"What made you say that?" Robin's question was quick.

"Oh," David Means said calmly, "that's the usual medium. But don't think I'm being callous. I called Jenny up and found out that Kitty had slept, eaten her breakfast and was feeling quite chipper. Now, my boy, let's hear your story and how you come to look as though you'd swallowed the bottle yourself. What are you shutting the door for?"

"Doctor's orders. I am to tell you the whole truth, be sure no one overhears and then never repeat it to a living soul."

David looked surprised but waited until Robin was seated.

"All right. Go ahead. I'm past being shocked at anything and my lips are sealed, of course."

When Robin had finished his story, David Means's face also looked pale. He cleared his throat but said nothing for a full minute. Then slowly he nodded his head.

"I think I've got it."

"Oh, what?"

"I'm afraid someone is trying to make it seem as though you were in a hurry to get the wills probated."

"But of course. I thought of that at once. That's why I'm

so scared. I'm terrified, really, for I'm completely helpless."

David Means suddenly held out his hand, with a smile. "Robin," he said, "I don't believe you could practice deception if you tried. You're a transparently honest man and I may add I'm glad you and Alice are still managing to see each other."

"That brings up something else, as though I hadn't enough to worry me. I went to the kitchen last night for a cup of tea. Poor Molly! I don't think she ever knew a young man before and she thinks she's in love with me. It was pretty awful for she indicated her room and all that. I made myself clear and got her to sit down and have a cup of tea with me and she gave me her opinions of the squire, by the way, which were, to say the least, illuminating."

"I'll bet they were."

"When I got up to go she stood there with the tears running down her cheeks, the most pathetic object you can imagine, and I did feel sorry for her, so out of pity I just gave her a very light kiss on the forehead and turned quickly toward the door. And there stood the squire, taking it all in!"

"Oh, *no!*"

"Yes. Quite. And while I tried to explain with dignity, he only grinned in a very meaningful way and I realized I had been a fool to show my pity for Molly as I did, for he may use it against me somehow. My immediate worry is whether to tell Alice the whole thing. What do you think?"

"You've certainly been hit with both barrels, my boy, but I have a suggestion. Would you like me to tell her your experience with Molly *and* the squire and that you are very much worried about the whole thing? She certainly won't be jealous," and David laughed, "but she will appreciate your telling me, man to man, all about it. And I think you'll find she'll be very *gentle* with you the next time you meet."

"That would lift a load from my heart. Now we can get down to the detective work. What do you think of the mushroom story?"

"Not too bad. These crazy 'toadstools,' as the children call them, spring up every summer, in one place, right there at the foot of the sassafras bushes. I doubt if they are really poison but everybody thinks so, and every child is warned about them; we often see some out in our woods but I'd never take a chance on them and Hepsy wouldn't touch them with a ten-foot pole. But it's conceivable that in pulling up sassafras roots some of these so-called mushrooms might have gotten mixed up with them. It makes a fairly believable story and it's my opinion the town will swallow it."

"Yes, but what are we ourselves to think of the real thing . . . the . . . the arsenic? The doctor was going to check Charles's little greenhouse this morning to see if he had any powders he might be using for his flowers or his plants . . ."

"That could be. You can buy arsenic easily and he boasted to me once that he had made up a concoction that was death to bugs. But even if he had some of the stuff there, it would still have to get into Kitty's tea."

"We're blocked on every side," Robin said. "I feel desperate."

Mr. Means smoothed his neat moustache and stared hard

at "Washington Crossing the Delaware." "Well, there is this," he said finally, "that comes to my mind. All the vegetables for the house kitchen are first washed by Charles in his little greenhouse sink. The sassafras roots too, I would assume. Now let's imagine a little bottle of arsenic on the shelf above the sink being jarred a bit just when he was doing the sassafras? Could be, couldn't it? Just a little powder sticking to the roots would be enough to make her sick. It all sounds a bit lame but it's a *possibility* and that's what we need at the moment. What do you think?"

"I think you're a marvel and somehow my heart feels a lot lighter. We should still keep our eyes open, though, shouldn't we?"

"Heavens yes. Our great concern at the moment is the town. I'll discuss these ideas with Doc and then if he agrees we can quietly spread them for what they're worth. One good thing is that we won't have to tell *many* people to have the matter broadcast. And in a way it's a good thing."

"How's that?" Robin asked.

"Well, it's hard to explain. It's a matter of reaction really. When the whole town talks something over and over for about a month the result is they finally get used to the thought. The sharp edges soften up. They begin then to discuss other things. The catalyst has done its work. Not a bad idea."

Robin laughed. "You do me no end of good. If you could just tell me now how soon I can see Alice, I'll give you full marks for a detective and a philosopher to boot."

It was David Means's turn to laugh. "Not much of either,

I'm afraid, but as to Alice, it's been a little while now since she's had lunch with me, long enough to quiet her Victorian father's misgivings. When's your next day off?"

"Tomorrow, but even so, maybe I should spend it with Cousin Kitty. I couldn't just run out on her so soon, could I?"

"N — no, I hadn't thought of that, but you're quite right. However . . . we might do it this way. I'll invite Alice to dinner on some pretext, Hepsy's southern fried chicken for instance. You entertain the ladies all day and then tell them you're invited to have dinner with me. If you add that you think Alice is to be there too, they will rise to the plan like a trout to the fly. They are romantic, you know."

Robin's voice sounded a bit choked. "You're so good to me. I don't deserve such kindness but I can assure you I'll try to be worthy of it."

They talked then a little longer of the sinister side of the recent happenings and what or who was beneath them.

"Of course," David Means said, "we can write off Molly Hart to begin with. She would lie down and let the ladies walk over her if they wanted to do so. Then this Charles, how does he strike you?"

"Stupid," said Robin.

"Dumb is the word," Mr. Means went on. "Perfectly happy if he can work in the garden without anyone to bother him. He likes flowers and he grew almost lyric once when he described how he killed potato bugs. He likes to attend to the horses and is as content with life as anyone I ever saw. I think we can rule him out."

"No one else in the way of help, then."

"Just one, as far as I know. Mrs. Alder, always emphasis on the *Mrs.,* who comes once a week to clean house. She's a sort of preacher-elder in a small church sect in the other part of town. She's *very* religious according to her lights and very unobtrusively devoted to the ladies. They haven't left her or her church any money for they once told me so and said they had explained this to her but will help her with her special offerings. I'm sure she's out."

"That leaves the squire and me," Robin said grimly.

"And me," said David.

"How you?"

"Oh, you could make quite a case against me. Old family friend, jealous at being overlooked, works upon the feelings of the sisters and gets them to change their wills in his favor. Under a bland exterior he's really a villain and makes attempts upon their lives . . ."

Then he stopped suddenly and his face looked drawn.

"I may seem to speak lightly, Robin, but under it all I am terribly worried and frightened. After I talk to Doc I'll know whether he thinks our arsenic story will hold water. If not, we'll have to stick to the mushrooms. It won't be hard to spread either story or both. But I think there will have to be a more careful watch on your cousins for a while at least until we are sure these happenings have been pure coincidence. And damn it, they just may be at that! Stranger things have happened in this old town. As to keeping a sort of watch, maybe you could leave your door open at night. I don't think Molly will bother you," he added laughing.

"Then I'll get my daughter and Alice, too, to join me in frequent calls to check on them. And try not to worry, Robin. You're as innocent as I am, so just stick to your job and go on your normal way."

"You haven't cleared the squire," Robin said gravely.

"Oh, him!" Mr. Means replied with a smile. "He's a gossipy old fuss-budget who likes to stick his nose into other peoples' business, but I doubt if any sort of crime would be in his line. I'm sure he's enjoying the present circumstances to the full, however, and we'll have to get our special rumors to him as fast as possible. Well, I'll get on to catch Doc if I can before he gets too far away on his calls, and you get on to your work and don't forget about dinner tomorrow night."

"As if I could, and thank you again. I forgot to tell you the squire said he would be watching me."

"Let him!" David Means said and with a final wave of his hand went out the door.

Robin worked hard that morning at transferring the contents of one old book into a new one, slow, meticulous columns, calculated to keep his mind off his anxiety. He did think between times of Alice and the joy of seeing her tomorrow evening. How could he help doing that? Just before noon the phone rang and David Means's voice came calmly over the wire.

"Robin? You know that matter we were discussing seems to be all right. Also about dinner. Hepsy suggests five-thirty as she plans to drive out to see her cousins just after. She's a good driver and will take Molly Hart with her. So, I guess that's all. Just give my regards to any inquiring friends."

Robin laughed as he hung up the phone. What a master of innocent subterfuge the old gentleman was. He had evidently checked with the doctor and both mushroom and arsenic explanations were to be used. Robin himself was to spread the word to all who inquired. Also due to the absence of Hepsy and Molly tomorrow evening he and Alice were to have precious time alone. All this was in the message which Hepsy of course would strain to hear and then decide had nothing interesting in it.

That evening in the Adair house all was normal except that Miss Kitty looked a little pale and Molly Hart unaccountably flushed.

"And you'll be home all day tomorrow?" the cousins asked in a breath.

"All day. I'll be at your service. Mr. Means has asked me to dinner. Would you mind? He's asking his granddaughter too."

The two old ladies looked at each other with romance lighting their eyes. "Oh, no!" said Miss Jenny, "we wouldn't mind at all. That will be so nice for you and Alice . . . I mean you need to see young people and there couldn't be a lovelier young girl than Alice for you to . . . I mean to associate with."

"And besides," put in Miss Kitty, "she's David Means's granddaughter and that makes it all seem so . . . well you know, so *right*. No, we won't mind your going at all when it's with Alice, I mean when it's at David's house."

"I'm afraid it will be a bit early. Hepsy suggested five-thirty. I think," he added as Molly came in to collect the after-dinner coffee cups, "that she has some idea of taking you along for a ride, Molly. Mr. Means says she drives well. That would be fun for you both, wouldn't it?"

Molly pursed up her lips. "Well, I could think of things that would be *more* fun," she said, "but I'll go along with whatever she wants to do. What are you going to do, Mr. Robin? Just sit and talk with Mr. Means all evening?"

"Oh, no," Miss Jenny said quickly. "Miss Alice is to be there too."

Molly made a quick movement and dropped a cup. Her face was scarlet. "It didn't break," she defended. "I just turned too quick."

When she had gone Miss Kitty looked worried. "I don't know what's got into Molly," she said. "She seems nervous and sometimes she's even irritable. She never used to be like that."

"Oh," Miss Jenny returned, knowingly, "she's perhaps just a little self-conscious with a handsome young man in the house. She's so completely shy and reserved."

"Dear me," agreed Miss Kitty. "That might just be it, though I never would have thought of it. You're so clever, Jenny."

Robin dressed for dinner with the greatest care. It was actually a short time since he had seen Alice but it seemed to him like a year. He kissed the cousins good-bye with tenderness and whispered to Miss Kitty that he would leave his door open that night.

"Oh, what a relief that will be!" she said. "I'm perfectly all right now but I love to think you're within call."

Robin pondered on the new plan as he drove to Mr. Means's. He was not at all eager to leave his door open at night. There just might be complications. Of course, he thought, he could put a chair across it, then any movement would wake him. Or would it? He was normally a heavy sleeper. In any case he couldn't very well refuse and was probably just imagining things about poor Molly.

When he arrived at the white house on the edge of the woods he found his host on the porch with Alice, bewitching in a white dress with blue sash, beside him. It was hard to say only the conventional words to her when his heart was overflowing with love, but he managed to greet them both with some show of normal expressions before dinner was announced.

"If you haven't tasted Hepsy's southern fried chicken, you are about to have a delicious surprise," Alice remarked as the plates were served, and Hepsy passed them, beaming.

There were many encomiums as the meal progressed; and Hepsy departed at last, all smiles, when her kitchen work was done to hitch up the horse and start for her ride. They all waved her off, and then when the golden light streamed across the porch Mr. Means found he must have a certain book and went off to his study to find it. He did not return, as the young people knew he wouldn't, and they were at last alone in each other's arms.

"I haven't slept these last two awful nights," Alice wept.

"Neither have I. But dearest, you mustn't be so saddened by all this. You surely know I've done nothing wrong."

"Of course, but the stories people are telling hurt me in *here*," she said, touching her heart. "And George is the worst," she added, breaking down again.

"Yes, I can imagine," he said. "But now, listen. I'll tell

you what the doctor and your grandfather are telling and they've asked me to say the same thing."

He told her then, of the chance of the bad mushrooms getting mixed with the sassafras; also of the bottle of arsenic in the greenhouse with the possibility of its slight spill over the roots as Charles was getting them ready to take up to the kitchen. Alice raised her clear gray eyes to his. "Do you really believe either of these stories?"

"No," Robin said quietly, "I don't. But we hope if they're told often enough, the town will. They will be given only as *possibilities* of course and that will leave room for debate back and forth which will give people a lot to talk about."

"But if neither of these possibilities is true, and they both seem doubtful to me, how did it really happen? Who did it? Oh, Robin, I can't bear to see you under suspicion. In the first place," she ended stoutly, "it's so ridiculous!"

They both laughed, which broke the tension. "That's the way I feel," he said. "How could anyone believe for a minute that I would willfully harm the old cousins? And besides that, you'd think they'd credit me with enough intelligence not to go about it all in such a clumsy way. Of course poor George — I honestly feel sorry for him — might clutch at any straw to get me out of the way."

"And the squire?" Alice said with a small laugh.

"Oh, *him!* I don't think he likes me and he's by nature suspicious, but his main interest now is in having a choice bit of news to impart to all and sundry. Can't you just hear him whispering to a customer, 'Another accident out at the Miss Adairs. Miss Kitty was *poisoned* last night! No clues, but it don't look good to me!' That's all he need say to start a chain reaction. Well, let's forget the whole thing now. I have you here, all to myself. You believe in me. My conscience is clear, so let's make the most of our precious time."

When the first sweet embraces were over Alice picked up the small book of poems her grandfather had left for them. "This is for you but he thought we might enjoy a few together," she said. "It's a sort of anthology. Oh, Robin, are you going on with your writing?"

"When I can get my mind settled enough. I haven't heard from the two pieces I've sent out, but it may take some time. Let's see the book."

He leafed through it and then drew her head against his shoulder as he read slowly from favorites here and there, often repeating lines that particularly impressed them.

At one time he laid his hand on her shining hair as he kept quoting:

> Shine out, little head sunning over with curls
> To the flowers and be their sun.

"Oh," Alice breathed, "read the last lines of those verses. The ones you like so much."

So Robin gave them without looking at the book:

> She is coming, my own, my sweet;
> Were it ever so airy a tread
> My heart would hear her and beat
> Were it earth in an earthy bed;
> Would start and tremble under her feet,
> And blossom in purple and red.

Dusk came on gently and the swing moved back and forth slowly beneath them. A full orchestration of crickets came from the grass and bushes. There were no sounds from the street. The two young people sat on in each other's arms, content.

"I'm glad we read the poems," Alice said at last. "They just seemed to be made for our evening together. All but the last one," she added. "It made me shiver a little."

" 'The Sands of Dee'?"

"Yes. It was sad."

> Oh! is it weed, or fish, or floating hair . . .
> Above the nets at sea? . . .
> Was never salmon yet that shone so fair
> Among the stakes on Dee.

"I fished in the Dee once," Robin added, "when my father and I were on holiday. It's a lovely river. I'll tell you about it."

"Oh, do. And we've never discussed the corn roast! There is so much to say, isn't there?"

"There never will be time enough to talk until we're married. Do you think the latest 'accident,' as the squire calls it, will make your father more set against me?"

"I don't know. I'll tell the stories the doctor wants people to hear and I'm sure Tom will. I'll explain them to him when he comes for me tonight."

"To think I can't even drive you home!" Robin said, a trace of anger in his voice. "But I shouldn't complain after having you with me all evening. I do feel discouraged sometimes as I look ahead to the winter's coming. It seems like a long, dreary waste to me when I have to wait."

"But you mustn't feel that way. I'll tell you how the weather is in Callaway. The autumn always seems to be over quickly and the snow falls soon. Then all the men get out their sleds and cutters and shine up the sleigh bells and the whole town is one constant chime. I don't believe you've ever heard anything like it."

"I don't believe I have."

"Then before we know it, with all the sleigh rides and parties, it's Christmas and then, all at once before you could think it's possible, it's *spring!* And I'm hoping by then . . ."

He bent over her blushing face. "What, darling?"

"I'm hoping father will have a change of heart by that time."

"Even after what has just happened?"

Alice held her head up and her eyes were bright. "Yes, I think this will all blow over like the carpet episode. I know it's worse but if enough people are casual about it and go on as before . . ." she drew a quick sigh ". . . we've got a good chance," she said.

Then they talked of the corn roast and the fishing in the Dee until Tom appeared at the steps and Mr. Means sauntered in from the library.

"I believe," the latter said, looking at his grandson, "that this might be a good time to explain what the doctor thinks happened to Miss Kitty, eh Robin?"

"Yes, I do."

So Mr. Means told it all quite simply and plausibly while Tom stared at a spot above his grandfather's head. "And this is what we are all to say?" he asked.

"Exactly."

"Well, I can readily believe the arsenic part, for I know Charles keeps little bottles of powder along the greenhouse shelf and uses them to make concoctions for his plants. I doubt the mushroom tale but I'll throw it in for good measure. Do you think the town's going to swallow this, Grandfather?"

"Wouldn't be surprised, if we're all casual enough."

"We may have to muzzle the squire, though," Tom said. "I was in his shop for a newspaper this evening early and he had several people round him. He was laying it on with an air of great mystery. Sinister, of course."

Mr. Means jumped. "I suddenly stand in great need of the world's news," he said. "I'll go up and get a paper and you young folks stay as long as you please and come back whenever you can. My house is yours. This is the squire's late night at his store so I ought to catch him. Thanks for the tip, Tom. Good night, my dear." He kissed Alice, picked up his hat, waved to the boys and was off.

"I'm glad he's gone," Tom said, "for the squire was certainly riding his horse when I was in. If anyone can pull him up a bit, Grandfather can."

When David Means reached the stationer's store he was amazed to see a small crowd of people collected around the squire, who was speaking in low tones to them as they drank in his words.

David did not wait to listen. "Hello, Squire," he called out cheerfully. "You seem to be doing a land office business to-night."

The squire looked up, anger written large upon his face. "David Means," he said, "I can't understand your levity when an old friend of yours may still be lying at the point of death by a *poisoner's* hand!"

David advanced toward the group. "Oh, come, come, Squire. I think you're making a mountain out of a molehill. If you refer to Miss Kitty Adair, I talked to her on the phone not an hour ago and she's as chipper as a cricket. As to what you call the poisoning, the doctor has found out all about that. Perfectly simple explanation. Let me have an *Evening News,* please."

The voices rose at once. "Oh, Mr. Means, tell us about it!" "What happened?" "We're so shocked." "Poor Miss Kitty!"

"Now listen, all of you," David Means said, turning about with his paper under his arm. "Miss Kitty did get very sick last night. She had sassafras tea for supper and no one else had. So at first the doctor thought there might have been some of those bad mushrooms gathered up with the sassafras roots. But a laboratory test showed a trace — just a trace — of arsenic in the stomach, so Doc set about finding it. And he did."

"He *did!*" came from all lips.

"Yes. It was quite simple. Charles keeps a little bottle on the ledge over his sink in the greenhouse to mix with other powders for his plants in the garden. He says he may likely have left it uncorked and some may have spilled into the sink. Even though he washed it out, enough of the rinsings could have stuck to the sassafras when he was washing *it*. So, there you have it. Plain as the nose on your face. Anyone coming my way?" he added, turning to the door.

Most of the group followed him, eager, he knew, to thrash it all over again. Which would be good. Behind them the squire's strident tones could be heard. "I ain't satisfied, I can tell you that."

As David Means strolled along, by his very pace indicating a serenity of mind, his neighbors also seemed to relax and their questions came with calmness. When one man laughed a little at the squire's excitement, David felt the day was in great part won.

"Oh, the squire's a good friend of mine," he said, "and I hope always will be, but he does get a little overwrought about small things."

"Like those tacks in the carpet," one woman said.

"Exactly. Well, you can just tell what happened this time as you have opportunity."

"Of course . . . that young man . . . that young Robin . . ."

"Nice chap," Mr. Means stated. "Keeps books, you know, for the hardware store and let me tell you," he lowered his voice, "they've never been kept so well before."

"But," the other persisted, "the squire says the old ladies changed their wills *in his favor!*"

"Wouldn't doubt it," said David. "You know about old Bessie Knott. They say she changed hers every week. Gave her something to do. That's the way with all old ladies. Oh, I wouldn't pay any attention to that. Well here's where I turn off. Just ask Doc if any of you aren't satisfied. Goodnight, my Christian friends!" And David Means walked jauntily up his street, while the rest of the group straggled on to their homes, deflated, with their former ebullient suspicions knocked out of them.

"I'll bet it was just as Dave Means said," one neighbor spoke to another.

"The squire always did like rolling a piece of news around his jaws. Well, we can see how the town takes this."

"And as to Charles, I've seen him pretty free with his bottles myself."

In spite of David Means's casual behavior in the squire's store and his walk from it, he lay the following nights uneasy and wakeful as did Dr. Brown, to whom broken sleep was customary. Their minds, both keen and trained to think in a straight line, now found themselves following a devious track. While the town, after much threshing of the problem in kitchens, street corners, the mill, the post office and the bank, everywhere, indeed where men and women gathered, had in the main come to accept the conclusions of the doctor and David Means, those two did not. In their inmost souls they sided with the small minority who still said, *"There's something behind this. Someone! But who?"* So they lay pondering, questioning, bringing one after another to the bar of justice only to exonerate all and send them innocently away. And yet as they met occasionally for a secret talk, the doctor would say slowly, "I'm convinced this was no accident." And David Means would answer, "So am I, but where does that leave us?"

The attitude of the town seemed incredibly better than those who best knew both it and the secret doubts had expected. In a few weeks Miss Jenny and Miss Kitty were serving tea in their big parlor as usual; they drove abroad in lovely mild afternoons; they not only attended church but also the play that the Masons gave in Patterson's Hall, with Robin escorting them to both. At those times the ladies themselves looked so happy and content and Robin so affectionate and solicitous that any last lingering doubts were dispelled from the public mind in regard to him, and the explanations seemed to grow more reasonable, more acceptable as remembrance grew more vague. And as though to provide its own quiet benison, the autumn covered the town with its crimson and golden glory.

Sometimes at their occasional precious times together Alice questioned Robin.

"Do you really think that everyone now accepts the story about the poison?"

He always hesitated a few seconds. "Well," he would answer slowly, "I think the squire likes to hang on to a mystery and of course George Hastings does a little talking, but in the main, people seem to be satisfied. What about your father?"

"I can't make him out," said Alice. "He doesn't mention you, or Miss Kitty or the incident at all. I think he has other troubles on his mind. There's been a little jealousy I hear among the bank officials. So we don't need to worry about him."

But as the autumn moved into Indian summer and a delicate haze drifted from the mountains to the valley, a new beauty seemed to fall upon the lovers. For one thing, every month brought nearer the great day when they would at last be one. It had been decided in their own minds that regardless of parental disapproval they would wait no longer than spring.

"Mother won't object and Grandfather will give me away even if Father won't, and oh, won't Miss Jenny and Miss Kitty be pleased!" Alice kept saying, while Robin drew her closer.

As she had predicted to him, the fall passed swiftly and suddenly Thanksgiving was upon them with a generous light snow, more than was known as a "skift," covering the streets and fields. There had always been a close friendship between the Miss Adairs and the Newcombes so on feast days the two families had dined together in the big house time out of mind. On this day the big parlor fireplace was all alight with the logs Robin had carefully laid; there were great bowls of chrysanthemums which David Means never forgot; the squire, as a lonely bachelor, was always included and brought with him a box of candy which everyone tried not to think small for the occasion.

While the older people chatted around the fire, the young folks found work to do. Tom and Robin arranged the fruit centerpiece on the dining-room table and Alice went at once to the kitchen to help Molly Hart, who though more nervous than her usual stolid state, was still happy apparently to be a part of the general excitement.

"I always say your mother has no call to bring the mince pies! I can bake them as good as she can," Molly said once.

"Of course you can," Alice placated. "It's just that Mother likes to have a little part in the dinner. Look at all this that you've done yourself!"

So the waters were oiled and all went smoothly until the great bird was ready for the platter. Robin, who had been keeping an eye on the kitchen from the dining-room door, came out at once.

"I'll lift that, Molly. It's too heavy for you. It goes in front of your grandfather at the end of the table, doesn't it, Alice?"

"*I'll* tell you where it goes," Molly said sharply. "Come on with me. Alice can pour out the gravy."

As they entered the dining room she added in a low but audible voice. "It would be nice and friendly to keep your door open again. I like it that way."

Robin flushed to the roots of his hair. "You know I was doing that for Miss Kitty by the doctor's orders. There's no occasion for it now."

"Oh I don't know. There m . . . might be," Molly stammered.

Robin set the turkey down in its place and looked around anxiously to catch Alice's eye. But he was not successful. She was busy setting the rolls in the warming closet as Molly, straightening her apron, said, "Come along. We can announce dinner now."

In a few minutes the long table with its shining crystal and silver was filled. Miss Jenny, handsome and stately, sat at one end with David Means opposite. As to the others, Miss Kitty said with a spirited wave of her hand, "Won't the rest of you just dispose yourselves as you wish? We tried to make place cards, but we got so mixed up. Only Robin dear, will you please sit next to me, and perhaps Alice next to him. Now let's sit down, and Sister Jenny, who did you select to say grace? I can't remember."

"I hope our good friend, the squire, will favor us," said Miss Jenny.

"Delighted to be of service, I'm sure," said the squire, unctuously, folding his hands.

The grace was lengthy in the extreme. Everyone was a subject of petition — "and bless the dear ladies at whose bountiful board we sit! May no evil befall them or ill-wisher molest them." Tom and Robin exchanged glances with one another for the turkey, implying its heat might be dissipating; David Means cleared his throat decidedly several times but the squire's spiritual rhetoric apparently could not be arrested. When the *Amen* was finally reached, David echoed it distinctly and rose at once to carve the bird. He did this expertly, as he had done many other things in his life, and before long the large gold-bordered plates were all circulated and Molly was passing the other viands.

"Now, this is what I like," pronounced the squire, "just a good plain dinner with no frills."

"Oh, but we are having frills," Miss Kitty said. "We're having sherbet along with the turkey. It's the latest thing. You're bringing it soon, aren't you, Molly?"

"Soon as I can," she said, rather tartly. "I got to get the other things going, first."

"I always think of Uncle Job Harley when we have ices."

"*Great* uncle," Miss Jenny prompted.

"Well, *great* uncle then. He married one of the Harrison girls, Sarah, I think."

"It was Josephine," from Miss Jenny.

"What a memory you have! Well, the Harrisons were a fine family. A long line of preachers and professors and men like that. We were related to them through the McKinstries on the mother's side. But how this girl ever came to marry this old Job Harley we never could figure out. When people spoke of him they always put in that old saying that if he took a girl to the ice cream parlor he would order a five-cent dish with two spoons in it! He was so stingy and . . ."

"And the paper says we are to have more snow," David Means cut in decidedly. "A regular old-fashioned winter. Ah, here is the sherbet," as the little cups were set at each place. "What a refreshing idea, and the latest fashion too, you say. Do you serve ices this way in England, Robin?"

From that point on the young people, taking the bit in their teeth as it were, kept the conversation on a light, even gay note, gently fending off any attempts at long, genealogical reminiscences from the old ladies or town gossip from the squire, aided and abetted by David Means, who had an uncanny gift for interjecting a perfectly polite but silencing remark when needed.

When the last bit of mince pie had disappeared amid expressions of pleasure and congratulation for the whole dinner, David stroked his ample waistcoat and exclaimed, "A child could play with me now!"

Then laughing, they all repaired to the drawing room for music. But here Robin demanded that Miss Kitty play first. "Any vocalizing from me after that dinner would be just impossible for a while," he insisted.

So Miss Kitty, pushed and flattered, sat down at the grand piano as Tom poked the logs into a new flame, and gave her small repertoire, dreaming as she did of the days when her silk skirts were pink, not black, and it was she who had sat in the rose garden. Her eyes fell upon Robin as her youth seemed to return to her. *Dear boy,* she thought, *how much joy he has brought us,* and she ended her little recital with the Moonlight Sonata.

Miss Jenny spoke low to Alice. "I think we should ask Molly in to hear the music, don't you?"

"I'll go ask her," Alice replied.

She found Molly with the dishes neatly stacked, ready for washing. But to the invitation for the drawing room she turned a rather expressionless face.

"Did *he* ask me?"

"You mean Mr. Robin? No, he hasn't begun to sing yet. Miss Kitty has been playing."

"I have ears," said Molly.

"I mean it would naturally be Miss Jenny who would invite you," Alice amended.

"Well, just say I'd rather get my work done. Tell Mr. Robin to stand near the door and I can hear him fine there. And thank Miss Jenny."

So Alice went back, puzzled and considering.

At last it was time for Robin and he gave them his best. At the other young people's urging he tried, "Knocked 'em in the Old Kent Road." Miss Kitty was delighted but Miss Jenny said it sounded just a *little* bit unrefined and perhaps he could sing "Drink to Me Only with Thine Eyes" next. Of course he ended as always with the whistle song and no one could help noticing that his eyes met those of Alice as he ended:

> I'll come to you, my lad!
> Oh, my love, I'll come to you.

Mr. Means had a suggestion when the music was over. "If Charles is around to hitch up the horses, or even if he isn't, for I'm capable, why couldn't the young folks have a ride in the cutter and the rest of us in the double sleigh of which, I may add, I hold fond memories."

*"David,"* said Miss Jenny, looking embarrassed. Then she said quickly, "do you think there is enough snow to ride out into the country?"

"More than here, probably."

"Hooray," shouted Tom. "Let's go. Only Dad, may I use our own sleigh? Maybe Mr. Means would drop you and Mother off on your way back. O.K.? I do have a sort of engagement."

Everyone laughed and Mr. Newcombe, who never could see a fault in his son, agreed to the plan, only drawing his brows a bit as he considered that Alice would now ride alone with young Adair. I'll stipulate, he thought to himself, that we'll keep them in sight. There was general movement then while all put on their warm outer garments. The men went out to the stables on hunt for Charles and the women waited in the main hall. Mrs. Newcombe drew Alice's red fascinator hood closer about her daughter's face and made sure she had her mittens and muff.

"And remember," she said, "to have that young man keep *both* hands on the reins. Horses get very skittish these first cold spells."

"Oh, *Moth* — er!" Alice remonstrated.

At last they were off, Robin and Alice first in the smart cutter, Tom in his own freshly painted one, and last the big two-seated sleigh with Mr. Means driving and the Newcombes, the Adair ladies and the squire in the seats. There was much calling and laughing and waving of muffs, and then, in spite of Mr. Newcombe's suggestion, the sleighs separated and all went different ways.

For what seemed a long time Robin and Alice sat quiet with the buffalo robe tucked cozily around them, watching the pale sun on the fresh snow, listening to the chime of the two strings of small bells on the horse's harness. It was like a new heaven to them. They had never before felt so removed from the rest of mankind, so warmly close, body against body, so surrounded with beauty. The afternoon shadows began to make purple patterns on the white; the hemlocks on the edge of the fields stood proudly under their new crowns; while all across the countryside there seemed to be a wide freedom, a spreading mystery from the snow.

Robin spoke at last. "If I were trying to describe this to put into a poem I would say there was all around us a sort of luminous peace."

"That's just right," Alice agreed. "I feel it, though I wouldn't have thought of the right words. For once, indeed, I don't want to talk."

"Neither do I. Why should we? We are together and for a little while the world is ours. I have to kiss you, though."

Then they rode on happily quiet, deeply content, until at last in the first blush of sunset to the west they saw the little new crescent moon, a mere shaving of silver, and knew it signaled the time for them to return.

It was pleasant getting back to the stone house, for all the rest except David Means had gone, so the five of them in comfortable harmony could discuss the sleigh rides before the fire and then eat the sandwiches Molly had prepared for them.

"She's gone to be with Hepsy and her relatives this evening. They came out for her," Miss Jenny said. "I'm glad she's going to have a little fun and not all work today. She's such a faithful girl."

"Will she be back tonight?" Robin asked.

"Oh, yes. They always bring her home. Some times it's late but she has her own key."

So, the cozy hours passed until at nine as usual, David rose. "Now, you had Alice's company all afternoon, Robin, so I'll claim the privilege of driving her home tonight. A wonderful day it's been, dear ladies, like so many before it. Thank you again more than I can say."

"The flowers, David, are so lovely!" Miss Jenny said.

"Just a gesture," he answered, "but a very affectionate one. Now, Alice, if you will get ready . . ."

"I'll help you get your wraps," Robin said hastily, knowing that the dark corner next to the hall closet might hold its rewards.

"And I'll go out to speak to Charles. He said he would wait up until I left and have my sleigh ready. It's getting on in years like myself. Do you remember, Jenny, the time we upset in it?"

But before she could answer, he was already in the hall on his way out.

When the last sounds of the departing guests had died away Robin looked at the old cousins and said that bed was plainly indicated.

"I *am* tired," admitted Miss Kitty, "but it's been a beautiful day."

"I'll help you upstairs, one at a time and very carefully," Robin laughed.

"Sister Jenny first, then, for she's the oldest," Miss Kitty insisted.

One at a time they went, leaning heavily on Robin's strong arm. In their bedrooms the lights were lit, the covers turned back and their night clothes laid out by the faithful Molly. Robin surveyed it all carefully.

"And you're sure you are both all right now? Nothing more I can do for you?"

"Nothing, dear boy. Just see to the downstairs, the fire, the lights and the doors. You look tired yourself!"

"I am, but only from enjoyment of the day. This has been my first Thanksgiving you know. We don't have this holiday in England."

"Why so you don't. Sister Kitty, did you hear that?" Miss Jenny called through the connecting door. "We should have made more of this fact at the table."

"I believe David did mention it. He always knows everything."

"Well, first or last," Robin said as he kissed them both tenderly, "it was wonderful and thank you again for all your kindness to me."

He went down the stairs deciding to have a cigar on the portico before he went to bed. The cousins did not approve of tobacco smoke in the house. The night air was sweet as he paced back and forth and so were the memories of the day, especially of those kisses in the snowy countryside when Alice's face, flushed and rosy as her hood, was raised to his own. He tossed away the end of the cigar at last and re-entered the house; there he checked the doors, smothered the last charring logs, placed the fire screen and put out the lights. He was glad Molly had her key so that he need not sit up for her, for he had to admit he was very tired himself. He went up to his room through the dim lights always left burning in the lower and upper halls, prepared for bed, climbed into the big fourposter and in five minutes was asleep.

It was much later when he woke suddenly. At least he had the feeling of having been asleep a long time. The small noise that had aroused him was the squeaking of the hinge on his door which he had meant for days to oil and had forgotten. He was lying facing it, his face half covered by the blanket, but he could see in his doorway against the dim light a figure clad in a white nightdress down to the floor. It was Molly. With something like terror in his heart he lay perfectly still, his breathing consciously heavy as though from sleep. She, too, was still for long minutes, then to Robin's horror began to move slowly toward him. He had time to wonder wretchedly what he would do. She was a strong little thing but naturally he was stronger. But if he should have to use force and in any way hurt her, whatever could he say to the cousins and what sort of story would *she* tell?

She spoke softly but he kept up his stertorous breathing, though he thought his lungs would burst. At last she turned around and went out with the hinge squeaking behind her.

Robin lay in a cold sweat.

"I'll have to put a lock on my door," he muttered when he got his breath normally, "for this is bad. It's *very* bad!"

## CHAPTER SIX

B UT THE VERY NEXT DAY something happened that drove all anxious thoughts from Robin's mind. He came home to lunch, an unassuming small lock in his pocket and a wrinkle in his brow, to find the cousins in a state of gentle excitement.

"There's a letter for you, Robin! We've never divulged the little secret you told us but we couldn't help seeing the return address. Here it is."

Miss Jenny held out to him the silver tray from the hall table where cards or letters were deposited. He took the thin envelope with a hand not quite steady, read the contents and suddenly sat down.

"Is it bad news? Oh, dear boy, don't ever be discouraged."

"No, no," he said. "It's uncommonly good news! I really wasn't prepared for anything so good. It's from the editor of *The Youth's Companion* and he likes my poem."

"Oh," Miss Kitty said breathlessly, "you know Sister and I have prayed over this. Is the letter . . . that is, could you read it to us?"

"Of course I can," Robin answered, his face beaming. "I'd like to hear the sound of it myself. Well, here it is:

Dear Mr. Adair:

We have considered the poem you submitted to us, and find it both humorous and charming. We are keeping it and a check for fifteen dollars will go forward to you next week. I hope you will send us further manuscripts. Have you thought of trying a boys' story? We are in need of such at the present.

With best wishes . . .

And it's signed by the editor himself! Oh, do you mind if I call Mr. Means right away?"

On the telephone he merely said he would stop in for a call after work and he wondered if Alice could happen in at the same time as he had a little piece of news to tell.

"Hooray!" came over the wire. "I think I can guess it. Stop work early for I can't bear the suspense and I'll have Alice here."

So at four, the three of them sat before the bright fireplace in Mr. Means's library and the precious letter was passed by hand to hand. David slapped Robin on the back and kept saying, "Well! Well! Well!" and occasionally "Hurrah"; Alice, after reading the message twice over, put her head down on the arm of the chair and cried for joy. Which of course demanded male comforting. But when her tears were dried and Robin had stopped smoothing her hair he spoke very seriously. "We really shouldn't be making too much of this. After all it's only a poem in a small magazine. I'm ashamed of my own exuberance but," he added ingenuously, "I am so terribly pleased."

"And so you should be," David Means said strongly. "Don't belittle your accomplishment. You've 'broken into print,' as the saying goes and that's no mean success. And while I don't know too much about editors I'm sure they don't ask to see more manuscripts unless they are really interested in the author. So, the thing for you, my boy, is to be as pleased as possible over this and go right on writing."

He eyed his young guests with a twinkle. "And just to prove how important I think this occasion is, I'm going to bring up a bottle from my cellar and we'll drink to this young fellow's career. But don't tell on me," he chuckled. "The Adair ladies do not approve of alcohol in any form, even champagne."

He poured the bubbling glasses and a close and happy mood fell upon them. Could the news be told? Alice wanted eagerly to know. The reassurance came quickly. This was one bit of information that need not be withheld from anybody.

"I'll have some fun with the squire," David said. "I'll tell him I've just learned something that perhaps he will want to keep to himself! That will insure its being broadcast immediately."

There was much laughter, for hearts were light. Alice sipped her one glass of champagne delicately, saying it was only the second time she had ever tasted it, but David Means and Robin finished the bottle like gay fellows and became almost the same age as they did so. When Robin said at last he must be getting back to the cousins, he wrung the older man's hand.

"I'll remember this always. Even if one day long ahead I write something important I'll always think of this celebration for my first little piece in print. And it was your encouragement that made it possible, sir."

"Tut! Tut! I'm happier than you. I'll drive you both back."

There was no doubt about it. While Callaway as a town was not at all averse to spreading bits of scandal and of course reveled in any news with a sinister tinge, it also delighted in pleasurable excitement and tongues wagged merrily. A first baby after a long marriage; an unexpected engagement of a couple past their first youth; the amazing recovery of one deemed hopelessly ill; all these and many more causes for rejoicing were made much of by the citizens. There was no doubt that the news of Robin Adair's poem accepted by *The Youth's Companion,* a magazine subscribed to by a number of families in the town, spread like wildfire. Nothing like this had ever happened before. Once in a while over the years there had appeared in the county paper a column or two on a local subject by a Callaway native, but this was very different. This would be the appearance of a poem in a national magazine which they all knew and respected. And this young Adair! Well, who would have thought it, watching him go quietly along the streets into his office, or squiring the old ladies on their peregrinations here and there. Why the plain fact was nobody had really appreciated him before. Just because he was a stranger they had been quick even to think ill of him. Now as with one accord they set themselves to atone.

"To think," one man said in the squire's stationery store, "that we have a *poet* in our midst and never knew it."

"Well," said the squire tartly, "I can tell you there have been plenty of poets no better than they ought to be."

"Why, Squire, aren't you pleased about this thing?"

"Oh, certainly," the squire backtracked hastily, "I was just stating a well-known fact."

"That's right, Squire," said David Means as he sauntered in for his paper, "you stick to the facts. They are that Robin Adair is a brilliant, gifted young man of whom Callaway may be proud."

In the general agreement the squire retired behind his counter irritated that David Means always managed to get the best of him.

But the man most affected by Robin's small success was Alice's father. After hearing the news from his family he began to find himself spoken to not only in the bank but on the street as well by men who usually began in some such manner as this: "Bill, I hear that pretty daughter of yours sees quite a little of this young Adair who lives with the old ladies. Well, he's sort of put the town on the map by getting his poem accepted, hasn't he?"

And one man even slapped Bill's shoulder and said, "You always know how to pick 'em and I guess it will be the same with a son-in-law!" He laughed loudly and passed on.

So Bill Newcombe had to realize that some of Robin's bit

of fame had actually passed on to him in the eyes of the townsfolk. But how, he wondered uncomfortably, could he possibly retire gracefully from the position he had held against him up to this time? It would be humiliating to have the boy feel that he, William Newcombe, was wanting to ride on the tail of the poetic kite. Never!

He pondered this for days while the town still discussed the matter happily and the Adair ladies served tea every afternoon to give greater opportunity to those who wished to hear the details again. Then suddenly Mr. Newcombe had an idea. At dinner one night after he had finished carving the roast, he said, "Alice, about this young Adair."

Alice jumped as though she had been shot.

"Yes, Father?"

"There seems to be a great deal of talk going on about this writing business of his. Now I never change my opinion in a hurry but I would be interested to know what he has written. Do you think he would come in some evening and read his poem to us?"

He had spoken very fast while Tom watched him shrewdly, his lips fixed in an apparent effort to hold back a grin. Alice turned white and then scarlet but her words were very clear.

"I'm sure he would come, Father, and appreciate the invitation. I'll ask him tonight."

"Oh, so you have kept on seeing him?"

"We had the ride on Thanksgiving, you know," Alice said gently, "and tonight Tom and Betsy and Robin and I were going out in the Miss Adairs' double sleigh."

"Well, that's all right, I guess. I'm never uneasy when Tom's along."

"Best chaperon in the state," Tom said with a side glance at his sister.

Charles brought the big sleigh in and said he would wait around with some cronies until the young people had returned from their ride. He warned them, though, that the country roads were badly drifted and it would be safer to stick to those in town and its environs.

Once again snuggled warmly under the buffalo robe Alice and Robin exchanged kisses and then she told the great news of the apparent softening of Mr. Newcombe's attitude. Robin was elated out of all reason. "It's the best result of my poem yet," he kept saying. "This may mean, that now we can see each other openly, and then *be married* openly. Oh, my darling, I'm so relieved and happy. Maybe I'm presumptuous but I hope he will like me. And if he approves couldn't I give you your ring for Christmas?"

Alice did not answer for what seemed to Robin a long time. "I would love it," she said at last, "but I'd rather wait a little longer, until Easter maybe. You won't think me morbid I'm sure but there have been strange difficulties before and I don't want to run into any more after I get my ring. I'll feel almost married then and I don't want any worries. But oh, I'll tell you what I *would* like for Christmas. A little round locket with a piece of your hair in it. Would that be too much?"

It was Robin's turn to be silent. He pressed her head

against his shoulder and she thought his eyes were wet upon her cheek.

"You would really like that?" he asked at last, huskily.

"Oh, so much. And I have thought of something for you that will be a complete surprise. Robin?"

"Yes, my sweet."

"Isn't it wonderful to be in love?"

They watched the beauty of the night around them. There had been more snow that morning and now there looked to be windrows of white along the eaves of the houses, while the lights shone like little hanging baskets of stars through the misty air.

They did not talk much except about Robin's writing, and as they watched the two heads in the front seat it looked as though conversation was not of prime importance there either.

Once Alice spoke hesitantly. "Robin, do you ever think about that strange *arsenic* business?"

"Well, yes. I do at times."

"I know Grandfather does and the doctor, but they have not come up with a single clue of any kind."

"Meanwhile the town seems to have accepted what it was told and questioned no further. I think we'd better let it go at that," Robin answered. "After all, the doctor's suggestion was a distinct possibility. When you spoke about not wanting to get your ring at Christmas, did it mean you have a kind of fear hanging over you? I couldn't bear that."

"Not exactly fear," she said, "it is just that we never talked it all over too much at the time and while naturally you are perfectly innocent I felt as though someone might be aiming indirectly at you. Oh, I know that sounds mixed."

"No," Robin said gravely, "it doesn't sound mixed in the least. I thought of the very same thing at the time, but now it seems vague to me, a sort of crazy idea. So, darling, please, *please* don't worry. I don't think anything further will happen and since I'm innocent I can certainly take care of myself. Let's just rejoice in our love and set a night for me to call upon your father. I'm terribly excited over this. Should I take more than one piece to read to him?"

They set two nights so Mr. Newcombe could choose; they discussed two poems; they spoke of how happy Alice's mother would be, and Tom, who had always been their ally.

"And be sure to sing," Alice urged, "especially 'Whistle and I'll Come to You, My Love,' for it's Mother's favorite."

Then for the last miles they were lost in the transports of their lovers' plans.

The night Mr. Newcombe set was Thursday of the following week. On that day Alice and her mother were very busy. There was serious discussion as to whether the fire should be laid in the front or the back parlor but it was decided that the back room would be more homelike, and besides, the piano was there. In addition to the reading of the verses, Alice set great hopes upon the singing to soften her father's heart. As the time approached Mr. Newcombe grew definitely irritable. It was as though he regretted his lapse from paternal Victorianism and in many ways made it clear he had not yet committed himself to approval of Robin. When the young man came, however, freshly groomed, smiling and, above all, modest, Mr. Newcombe thawed a trifle and shook hands almost with friendliness.

"Well, let's sit down now and hear this poem you wrote that's caused such a stir in the town, Mr. Adair."

"I'm ashamed of the stir, for it's only a small thing, but of course I can't deny, sir, that I'm pleased the magazine will print it."

"All right, go ahead. Let's hear it."

Robin drew some pages from his small portfolio and slowly read his poem. It was, indeed, the very description of the town he had once showed David Means, only now in verse. It was all there. The gentle running creek with its bending willows; the great matriarchal train with its flutter of admirers; the quiet citizenry bent upon their separate errands. And the poem closed with a brief description of the young men singing "Good-night, Ladies" on the steps of the ivy-covered brick houses.

When he finished there was complete silence, for he had read the lines with tender drama and the faces of the listeners showed it.

"Well, Well!" spoke Mr. Newcombe at last, "that's not bad. Caught quite a picture of the town I'd say. Not bad. Alice says you brought some more verses with you."

"Just one," Robin said. "It's a love poem, but of course every young man who wants to write tries his hand at this kind."

He read it slowly, his heart naturally in each word. When he finished Mrs. Newcombe was wiping her eyes, and her husband said again, "Not bad, that. Of course it sounds a little bit like a love-sick swain, but still, not bad. I would say, Adair, that you really have some talent for this sort of thing. Do you mean to keep on with it?"

"Yes I do, but more perhaps in prose. The editor wrote that they needed boys' stories."

"Good. That would be more in my line. Well, I hope you have success and I may say that I feel I know you a little better after hearing the poems than I did before. I may have been a bit hasty in my judgments. If you young folks enjoy seeing each other sometimes, I don't know why you shouldn't."

"Oh *Father!*" Alice exclaimed.

"Thank you, sir, very much indeed," Robin said, feeling that this was not the time for overenthusiasm. There was a general brightening of the atmosphere, however, as the songs and then the refreshments followed. Mrs. Newcombe had to hear the "Whistle and I'll Come to You, My Love" the second time, and Alice's cheeks were pure rose as she listened.

When Robin left, even Mr. Newcombe had the grace to say his good-bye in the parlor and allow Alice to show the guest to the front door alone. Here they had a brief, fervent embrace over the good news and there was nothing but warmth in his heart as Robin stepped out into the snow.

But when he reached home he found the sisters awake and tremulously glad to see him.

"We've been just a little frightened," Miss Jenny said, "and Sister Kitty was once almost in a faint but I used smelling salts and she recovered quickly."

"But what happened?" Robin asked. "Tell me at once."

"Noises," she said. "The strangest noises. First a great pounding on the back door, though Molly said when she answered no one was there. Then the front doorbell rang and rang. But she found no one there either. Then a little later there were queer, distressing calls like someone wanting help, but no sight of anyone. Molly put on her coat and looked all around and wakened Charles in the coach-house, and he could see nothing. Then everything was quiet again. And Robin, what do you make of it?"

"I think some bad boys were out on a spree and that all of this was a practical joke. I'd like to shake them all for frightening you so. How about Molly? How did she take it?"

"Oh, she was terribly upset, especially when Sister Kitty fainted. She was so white, you see, that Molly thought she was dead. I was wondering, Robin . . ."

"Yes, Cousin Jenny?"

"Do you think we could all keep our doors open tonight? When we are still a bit nervous. Would you mind?"

He swallowed stiffly. "Not at all. Would you like me to sit up down here?"

"Oh, I'm sure that won't be necessary if we just know you're within call. And even though it was hard on us, I'm glad you feel the evening's problems were just a joke."

"I don't," said Miss Kitty. "I believe it was a poor wayfarer in the snow seeking a haven and we didn't hear in time. It makes me sad."

"Now, don't worry," Robin said. "There are plenty of

other people living near if anyone needed help. Just put this down as a boys' prank and forget it. Has Molly gone to bed?"

"Yes, poor child. She had such a shock over Sister Kitty and of course she had been looking all around in the snow. Very brave of her. I'll speak to her when we go up. By the way, Robin, do you have to go out tomorrow night?"

"I don't have to go out any night if you need me," he answered.

"I was thinking if you could be at home until we get over our nervousness a little it would be a great comfort. And we haven't had a real visit from Alice, the dear child, for a long while. Perhaps she would spend a little time here and you would have young company to brighten the evening."

"Wonderful!"

"Well, we will consider it. And now, Kitty, it's time we got to bed."

Robin saw them safely to their rooms, received their gentle good-night kisses and went down to close up for the night. As he looked out of each door in turn he could see only muffled tracks such as he had made himself at the front, or Charles and the delivery boy could have made at the back. While it still seemed to him like a boyish prank it wasn't a nice one, and once again he had to face the fact that all the untoward happenings had occurred just since he, himself, had come. As he climbed the stairs he could hear Miss Jenny's voice along the hall. "And we are all leaving our doors open tonight, Molly, so you must be sure to."

Robin did not know whether to laugh or swear as he

heard the advice. He did the latter, however, when at some much later hour he woke to find Molly standing in his room. This time he did not hesitate. He threw on his dressing gown, went to her and caught her firmly by the arm.

"Now Molly," he said, "this has got to stop. I don't want you ever to come into my room again or I'll have to take harsh measures. Now, I'll stand here until you go through your own door. And then *stay* there!" he ended sternly.

"You haven't got no heart," Molly sobbed.

"I've got common sense and I hope from now on you will have the same. Now go on back."

Molly turned slowly, her sobs still audible. When she was half way along the hall Miss Jenny came out of her room.

"Why Molly, child, what's the matter?" She went to her and put her arm around the girl's trembling body.

Robin spoke quickly. "Molly is still nervous and upset. I think she was rather confused when she got up and I was going to watch here until she was safely back in her own quarters. Now, she will be all right, when you are with her. If you need me for anything, Cousin Jenny, do call."

But in a short time all was quiet, except for the soft beat of fresh snow upon the windowpanes, and in the morning a general peace prevailed as though no strange noises had disturbed the night. There was a hearty breakfast with Molly, her eyes modestly downcast, bringing her famous muffins to the table. "The body needs so much more sustenance in winter than in summer," Miss Jenny said as she helped herself to a third muffin. "Do eat well, Robin."

When he left for his office the cousins both bade him good-bye with a brightly conspiratorial air.

"And as soon as I think Alice and her mother are up and about, I'll attend to . . . you know what!" Miss Jenny said.

"And good success!" Robin wished them, as he set off for the drifted driveway, whistling, where Charles waited to drive him safely to town.

It was hard to keep his mind on account books that day. The weather itself was ominous with a gray sky growing heavier by the hour. All the wiseacres who watched from their doorways or waded through the streets in their heavy boots to discuss the matter with friends, agreed that there was going to be more snow. A premature dusk began to settle about three o'clock, and at four Charles appeared with the sleigh saying Miss Jenny had ordered it for it looked to them all as though they might be shut in for a while. He had done some shopping first and all the extra space of the sleigh was filled with bags and grocery packages.

Robin's heart sank. "Is . . . is . . . I mean is anyone else there?" he stammered.

"Lord yes, we're goin' to have a houseful all right if we do get snowbound. Miss Alice, she come out early and they asked her grandfather to bring her so he's there too. He brought a little satchel so I'll bet he's lottin' on spendin' the night anyway. He cocked his eye an' he says to me, 'Charles,' he says, 'unless I'm a monkey's uncle there's a big snow up there waitin' to come down on us.' An' he's a pretty wise man, when it comes to weather."

"What about you in the coach-house? Will you be all right?"

"Oh, Miss Jenny's got that all fixed too! I'm usually fine there with my oil stove but she says the way things may be for a few days I'm to move into the little garret room above the kitchen. I'll be right there you see to bring in the wood an' clear the walks an' that, an' I'll not be gettin' asphyxiated with the oil fumes like I might if I was all snowed in. Miss Jenny, she's quiet but she's a manager all right!"

"But all this sounds *wonderful!*" Robin burst out, drawing a great breath of the clean moist air. "You can't imagine what this snow is going to do for us!"

"Good for the crops," Charles replied.

What a welcome! Robin thought to himself as he finally reached the great parlor, having entered by way of the kitchen to divest himself of coat and boots. For they all rushed to greet him and draw him nearer the blazing hearth, the old cousins tremulously happy, David Means, his eyes wrinkling over the surprise of his visit, and Alice . . . ah, here, Robin stopped and suddenly bent his head over hers in view of them all. So if any vestige of a secret remained, it was now dissipated and the lovers stood, declared, before them.

Those three days of what the Callaway citizens were ever after to refer to as the Big Fall, were hours of pure joy in the stone house. Secure from all intrusion, wrapped in heaven's own soft but implacable covering, the great logs burned, the voices rose and fell happily and the thrill of young love sent a pulse of warm delight through the moving hours. As long as they lived Robin and Alice were to remember those brief, perfect days.

David Means was in high feather. The situation suited him exactly. At dinner he declared his pleasure over again, as he beamed upon them all.

"Now this is just what I've been needing, a real little visit. I've been poking about too much at home. Why, come to think of it I haven't been anywhere lately, not even to church."

"Now David," Miss Jenny said reprovingly, "for such a wise man and a student like you I think you take theology too lightly."

"Now how can you say that, Jenny, when, for example, I've been practicing *total depravity* all my life."

Robin led the laughter and the others joined, though Miss Kitty admitted she never was quite sure just what David meant. But the fun continued mildly but pleasantly around the fire later. There were songs and snatches of old stories and riddles and a few games, all punctuated by the entrance of Charles with fresh logs and reports on the weather.

"She's a-comin' down all right. Man and boy, I've never seen a snow like this one. I hope you've got enough grub laid in to eat, Miss Jenny."

"I think we've plenty of food," she answered with dignity.

By the next night the town was wrapped in silence and the drifts were growing higher. After dinner David brought down a little book from his satchel and explained that he was going to do something he had always wanted to do, with an audience. He read aloud Whittier's *Snow-Bound* quietly, movingly. And when he had finished and closed the book no one spoke. Robin finally broke the silence.

"Thank you, Mr. Means. You wouldn't quite know how much that meant to me, for I was hearing it for the first time. As an English schoolboy, I didn't happen to read it. It's very beautiful."

With David Means's discernment and tact he had managed each night to engage the old ladies in conversation just after they had announced that they felt bedtime had come now *for all*. So Robin and Alice in the dimness of the backhall, or perhaps behind the heavy damask curtains in dining room or library on pretext of watching the weather, had been able to exchange the long kisses in which their souls seemed to melt and become one.

"Will there ever again be such a happy time as this?" Alice whispered once.

"Much happier, I hope," Robin answered.

Then suddenly on the third day there appeared a misty circle in the eastern sky which gradually grew in brightness until in its center there was a scintillating ball which in its turn became the sun! It shown down benignly upon the white world. Its warmth grew until it seemed not only to begin the long process of melting the snow but to act upon the citizens of the town as well, who, freed now from their temporary hibernation, emerged from their houses with shovels and various implements and with much shouting back and forth began to make narrow pathways between the white walls. Some heavy sleds broke tracks through the main streets and the squire, watching anxiously from his shop door, called to a neighbor that he wouldn't be a bit surprised if the Old Girl would be able to make it by another day. "When she don't run it seems like the world's stopped," he added.

"That's right," called his neighbor.

Out at the stone house, Robin donned the proper clothing and armed with a shovel went out with Charles to dig through the drifts. It was heavy going but by afternoon they had a good path to the stables where the horses had been left with plenty of hay and some oats. Charles replenished their boxes and then, outside, looked the landscape over.

"No use even thinkin' of getting the sleigh out," he said. "We'll just have to leg it till the drive melts some, but we can clear off the porch an' the short walks a little."

By the next morning there broke upon the still air the melodious sound of bells, and the sun, as though to atone for its absence, shone down with fervent heat. Great cascades of snow came down from the roof with heavy thuds and the men's shovels found their white burden easy and yielding. Charles even began by noon to attack the drive.

"I've been lazy long enough," Robin said at lunch. "I think I should try to walk in to the office and do a little work. I won't stay late."

The cousins raised outcry at once and David Means settled it. "Not today, Robin. The game wouldn't be worth the candle. There's nothing in such need of you there. By tomorrow we may even be able to get the sleigh out. I ought to be getting home myself and be there when Hepsy gets back. She went to her aunt's. But my dear old friends, I must tell you again that this visit has been like an oasis in the desert for me!"

"For us too," Miss Kitty echoed. "I don't know when I've had such a good time. And so many laughs," she added.

So all afternoon Robin and Alice played Parcheesi at a little table by the library window and if hands touched often and eyes were not too much on the game, there was none to see or censure.

Alice had repeatedly offered her help to Molly but had as often been refused. Molly looked tired and as Miss Kitty said, "acted grumpy," but continued to produce superb meals and even though she set the plates down more energetically than was necessary those at the table only smiled and let it pass.

Tom called to say the farmers had driven their big sleds into town and it was amazing how clear the streets were, while many men and boys of all ages had made most of the sidewalks quite passable. So it became definitely the last night of the visit. When bedtime came and the others had gone up, Robin made his careful rounds and then went upstairs whistling. He, too, could never remember as happy a time as this in all his life.

He woke with a voice in the hall, and went at once to see what the trouble was. David Means stood in his doorway in a long tailed nightshirt and across from him was Molly, also in sleeping attire. Robin pressed closer in the shadow and listened.

"What's the matter, Molly? I say, what's wrong? What do you want?"

No reply.

David leaned comfortably against the door jamb as though for a chat. "You know you've done a wonderful job with the cooking, Molly. Don't you ever tell her but I do believe you can beat Hepsy. And there's been a crowd of us here. You must be tired to death. Aren't you?"

No answer.

"Well, sometimes when I'm clean done out, I get up at

night and walk in my sleep. Crazy thing to do, but a lot of folks do it. Now I believe that's what you did just now. You aren't scared, are you?"

Molly spoke at last. *"Scared!* Me? I ain't afraid of nothin'."

"Good. Well, you just go on back now to your room then and I'll stand here and watch till you get there. Miss Alice and I are leaving tomorrow so you'll have fewer to cook for. Now get along and have a good rest. Good-night, Molly."

The girl turned and slowly went down the hall, entered her room and shut the door. Fortunately the cousins were quiet. Robin stepped out and stood close to David Means. The older man eyed him shrewdly.

"Any trouble before with this?"

"Some," said Robin.

"Well, for the love of the Lord watch out. That girl's got a queer look in her eye. Always had, for that matter. I was lying awake and heard a soft step in the hall and thought I'd investigate."

Robin laughed. "I hope you didn't think it was mine."

David smiled. "No. Actually I thought it was likely Jenny going down to check on the fire. I've been here before when she's done that."

"In any case I'm glad you were here tonight, sir."

"So am I, and take care. 'Hell has no fury like a woman scorned.'"

"You can be sure I'll be careful. It's been a wonderful time these days, hasn't it? God bless the snow."

In the morning it was possible to get the sleighs out.

David Means, with his satchel, gave his heartfelt thanks to his hostesses; Alice, with her bags, kissed them warmly and told them with tears what the snowbound days had meant to her; Robin tucked her safely in beside her grandfather and then, with Charles driving him, followed in the family sleigh. They proceeded slowly but the sun as well as the farmers' sleds had done the work of excavation well and softly in track or through melted snow the runners found safe passage until they reached town where the tall banks still bordered streets and sidewalks.

Anyone could see, however, that the warm sun shining on the steel rails of the train tracks had left them burnished clean, and many a townsman said with relish, "I'll bet the Old Girl will make it today."

The Big Fall did not last. In a surprisingly short time the white walls crumbled, the weight on the roofs disappeared, and the streets became a dark and sodden slush. There had been great hope expressed by the young people that the snow would lie until Christmas, but having given this unprecedented abundance already, it was as though the elements felt there was no need of further effort on their part. So, disappointingly enough, there was no merry chime of bells over the holiday season, and the squire quoted darkly to his customers, " 'A green Christmas makes a white graveyard,' they say. For my part I'd rather see a *little* snow."

But with happiness in their hearts such as Alice and Robin knew, the weather did not matter much. On Christmas Eve in the Newcombes' own front parlor, where Robin was now welcome, they exchanged their gifts, which made their engagement seem complete even without the ring. Alice's locket bore on one golden side Robin's entwined initials and on the other, her own and when the lid sprang open there lay a small round of hair just fitting the space.

"I felt a little foolish putting that in, but you asked for it," he said, apologetically.

"I love it," she answered. "It's a real part of you I'll be wearing. Oh, Robin, thank you more than I can ever say. It's so very beautiful!"

Her gift to him was a thick gold watch fob and they laughed over the similarity of their tastes for it, too, bore his initials on one side and hers on the reverse. It had a carved border around the edge and was truly elegant. He fastened it to his chain at once and paraded about the room, hands in pockets so the fob could be fully seen.

"I've never had one before and now I'm proud as Punch. Even if I'd bought it myself I would have been enormously pleased with it, but when it's a gift from you . . . Oh, my darling!"

So Christmas was ushered in by two happy young hearts.

They had dinner as usual with the Miss Adairs and gifts of all sorts from the little hemlock in the back parlor afterwards. Then the men, David Means, Mr. Newcombe, Tom and the squire startled the others with some songs, Robin abstaining because he didn't know the words. But after much preliminary harmonizing with heads close together, the results were surprisingly good even if the voices were a bit rough in spots. They sang "Aunt Dinah's Quilting Party" and "Jingle Bells," even without the snow. Then gathering confidence from the applause they wandered into "Soft O'er the Fountain" and "Come Where My Love Lies Dreaming" and retired, covered with laurels at last.

"But I didn't know you men *sang*," Robin kept repeating.

"Oh, we used to keep a few barber shop quartets going through the town," Mr. Means said. "Gad, I haven't raised my voice for years, have you, Squire? But after all this is the day for carols. How about it, Alice?"

So the young people sang all the ladies' old favorites and then at five o'clock excused themselves gracefully with many thanks and left, for a big supper party was in the offing at the Wilsons', in the country where the corn roast had been.

"Wouldn't you like to take the carriage?" Miss Jenny asked.

Tom and Robin agreed at once as Miss Kitty said archly that she rather supposed Tom would also be taking a girl.

"You just bet I will and a mighty fine one, too."

"Oh, we know Betsy," Miss Kitty said, her eyes twinkling, "and I wish you the very best . . . oh, I mean I just love a romance!"

On the way to the country Alice tried to explain about the party to Robin. "You'll find this is one of our winter sports, like the sleighing, but you'll soon catch on to it and I'm sure you'll like it. It's quite a little drive to the Wilsons' when the roads are bad," she added. "The snow would have made it all much easier."

"But we wouldn't have had our wonderful snowbound days then, so I'll take the mud now. Oops," he said suddenly, "these ruts are deep. Though of course it's very hard for me to do, I think I'll have to hold you closer!"

They got safely to the Wilsons' house at last, where kerosene lanterns were strung along the orchard fence to light the way. The girls went in by the front door and in a gay medley of chatter with their friends went up to the spare room to lay aside their wraps. The boys left their coats and boots in the back hall. In the square living room, tables were laid with bread and butter, cold turkey and preserves, coffee or milk as desired and an abundance of mince and apple pies. It was already six-thirty and after an hour the faint tune of a fiddle could be heard coming from the kitchen. Robin, glancing through the door, saw that the floor of that large room was bare and all furniture moved out of the way. The young people finished their pie, and moved quickly toward the sound of the fiddle. The musician, a tall, lanky individual in a plaid shirt and heavy pants and with a quid of tobacco in one cheek stood in a corner sawing away, a little off key to Robin's sensitive ear. The older Wilson boy took charge.

"Now get your partners and form a circle. I'll be the odd man in the middle. I thought we'd start with Pig in the Parlor and Skip Come-a-lu just for a warm-up. All right? Everybody sing now."

The circle was formed with hands firmly clasped and moved slowly around to the rollicking tune and the inelegant words:

> O, we kept the pig in the parlor,
> And it was Irish too!

At a signal the circle reversed itself and each boy grasped

hand after hand of the girls behind him, then once again the movement and the song:

Oh, we'll all go down to Rouses,
We'll all go down to Rouses

In a little while Jim Wilson signaled them to stop. "That's enough of the Pig," he called. "Get your partners for Skip Come-a-lu. I'll be the center man again for I have no date. All set?"

Robin realized soon that this was a different kind of game. The reedy violin took up the strain and the girls, for all the foolish words, sang prettily. Jim in the center chasséd across the space and took Betsy from her place, then swung her around and around over and over again, then steadied her at last and left her breathless in the center to choose a new mate. Meanwhile the excitement was rising. The boys, watching the swaying couple, clapped and called and stomped and the girls sang on above the thin sound of the fiddle.

Little red wagon painted blue,
Flies in the sugar bowl, shoo, shoo, shoo.
My wife's gone and I'll go too,
Skip come-a-lu my darling.

At first Robin was alarmed. How could he ever do what these other fellows seemed to do so easily? Then suddenly he realized it was much like he had done dozens of times in an English waltz, only here there was more room. He soon had a chance to try, for Alice had been in the center and now came over to choose him.

"I hope I can manage this," he whispered.

"Of course you can. Just swing me around."

He held her firmly and after one or two false starts they fell into perfect step and began slowly, gracefully to circle the space, turning and turning but always as in a dance. Even Robin himself knew it must look very different from the somewhat crude gyrations of the other boys. He knew that the stomping had stopped and the circle was apparently watching silently except for faint snatches of the song, very soft clapping and a rising crescendo from the fiddle. They kept on and a certain grace and elegance seemed to spring from the rough boards of the kitchen floor.

"When should we stop?" Robin whispered.

"I suppose soon, but I love it," Alice whispered back.

So at last he turned more and more slowly and then stopped. All at once there was real applause. Alice blushed and Robin looked embarrassed as they stood for a moment, surprised at the smiling faces around them. There were calls, but pleasant ones: "That was great!" "Where did you ever learn that?" "We'll all be afraid to follow you!"

But Robin soon learned that the high point of the evening was yet to come. As before, Jim Wilson took charge, suggested everyone rest for a few minutes and then conferred with the fiddler. Alice and Robin were still receiving the plaudits of the group for their part in the last game, but it was clear she was trying to explain something to Robin.

"This next will be different and I imagine new to you. Did you ever do a *square dance*?"

"Never."

"The fiddler calls out what each couple is to do and it's

really not hard. We'll stay out and watch for a while, though, until you see how it's done."

"Get your partners," Jim Wilson called, "and form your squares."

And then all at once the fiddler was calling, above his tune:

> First couple out to the right!
> Around that couple and take a little peek.
> Back to the center and swing your sweet.
> Go up the river and cross the lake,
> A left allemande and a grand chain eight!
> Hurry up gents and don't go slow
> And meet your honey with a promeno!

"Good heavens," Robin whispered to Alice, "I don't know what the man's talking about! I can't do this."

"Just watch a little longer, and don't worry. We don't have to do it at all."

But little by little the strange words of the fiddler began to make sense to Robin; he saw the pattern of the dance emerging and the rhythm got into his blood. His poetic soul was stirred by the tapping feet, the swinging, laughing bodies. Who could resist this youthful ebullience all to a disciplined cadence?

"I do believe I'd like to try, if I don't make a fool of myself," he told Alice at last.

"I thought it would get you," she said. "We'll go into the next set."

Jim Wilson saw to it that they were in a square with Tom

and Betsy, who welcomed them effusively and promised to steer Robin straight if he was uncertain. Then the music and calls began.

> The head couple lead out to the right
> And balance there so kindly,
> Then pass right through and balance too,
> And swing that girl behind you.

The calling went on and to Robin's surprise, with a little direction from the others, he kept up with the musical directions and became part of the gay, rhythmic group. After that, he and Alice never missed a set.

On the way home he was exuberant. "Why, I never knew such fun existed," he kept saying. "It's been the most wonderful evening. Will there be others like it, this winter?"

"The trouble," Alice explained, "is that it's not much fun in a parlor on carpets, so it almost has to be in the country where there's a big kitchen which can be bare for the party. And there aren't too many of those. I hope the Daltons invite us even if May and Bill are a bit older than the rest of us. They still like a dance."

"Well, we can hope," Robin said.

February brought a moderate snow, a sensible one, as the squire called it, heavy enough to call out the sleighs and set the bells ringing again but nothing like the Big Fall to keep people immured in their houses. And with the snow came the looked-for dance at the Daltons, to which most of the young people journeyed in large borrowed farm sleds, the bottoms soft with straw and cushions where the occupants sat under blankets and robes, the males, of course, with close and tender hold upon the girls they had brought with them, to stave off the chilly wind blowing over their heads.

There were several things this waning winter season which warmed Robin's heart. First and greatest of all, his love, fresh and new with each succeeding day. There was the small triumph of his expertness in the dances which caused much favorable comment. And in his office after hours and at the desk in his room late at night, he had been working on his boys' story and had now completed it. He showed it to Mr. Means first and then on a cozy evening in his library read it aloud to Alice and her grandfather together. It was a touching little story but there was humor in it, too, and as Mr. Means observed, it was all boy. He was enthusiastic, trying, however, to temper his praise to forestall any possible disappointment. Alice loved it and said so without any reservations. It was settled then that at once it was to be sent to the editor of *The Youth's Companion.*

"But don't expect a reply too soon," David Means adjured. "A story may take much longer to consider than a poem. So don't get impatient. But I tell you sincerely, Robin, that I consider it good work."

One day when the back of the hard winter had been broken and March had with a lamblike gentleness driven the snow and the chill air to flight; when the soft green was creeping delicately up in the willows, and the bulbs were rising in the flower beds; when something intangible assailed the senses with promise, Robin entered the stone house at noon to find the cousins fluttering over the silver letter tray on the hall table. It was Miss Kitty this time who craved the privilege of presenting to Robin another thin envelope with distinctive script in the corner.

"Please open it quickly, dear," she said. "We simply can't bear to wait much longer."

Neither could Robin. He didn't sit down but slit the envelope carefully, read the page and then gave a whoop of joy.

"They've taken my story! The editor says they like it and would be glad to consider another and *listen to this:* 'A check for fifty dollars will reach you in two weeks.' I can't believe it! It's incredible. And, oh, it's all due to you both for giving me a home over here and a chance to do what I was longing to try. How can I ever thank you?"

He caught them, Miss Jenny first and then Miss Kitty, kissed their wrinkled cheeks and swung them gently around while they laughed with delight.

"Now, you must call up David Means," they said in a breath.

"If you don't mind," Robin said, "I think this time I'll call Alice first!" Molly Hart in the dining room heard it all and her face darkened.

"He'll call Alice first," she muttered when she was back in the kitchen. "So he's sold a story now to the paper and there'll be another big fuss in town about it. Some folks are just gettin' too big for their britches, *I* say, but there might be ways to . . ."

She left off muttering and began to serve the lunch. To the animated details of the news from the old ladies, she maintained an expressionless silence.

But that night while Robin and Alice once more in David Means's library quaffed another toast to Robin's literary career, listening meanwhile to David's gentle warnings that he must be prepared for some disappointments in spite of the fact that his beginning had been phenomenally good, even then while the three laughed and rejoiced and planned together, while the soft air with the first freshness of spring in it blew outside, Molly Hart, walking beside her bosom friend Hepsy, now with a diabolic mixture of secretiveness and innuendo, laid the first stone, as it were, in the foundation of the tragedy that was later to come.

## CHAPTER SEVEN

S PRING MADE no delaying that year. As though to atone for the cold winter, March proceeded even to the end with lamblike demeanor, and April grew first mild and then pleasantly warm. The birds twittered, the ploughman's voice could be heard from the nearby fields, the creek began to sing again, and the winter's bright hearth fires, the banking snows and the jingling bells were forgotten as though they had never been. Suddenly, before anyone could believe it, least of all Alice and Robin, May, the month set for their marriage, was at hand.

But over the beauty, penetrating the fragrant sunshine, there lay a shadow. Robin, going about his work, his head full of the joyous plans of a bridegroom, knew nothing of this until one evening Tom asked him to go for a drive. Robin, surprised, accepted. A small fear crept over him as they turned into a quiet country road, for Tom had spoken very little on the ride.

"Is anything wrong, Tom? Is Alice not happy about our . . . our plans?" He felt he could restrain himself no longer.

Tom answered him very slowly. "There is something

wrong and I don't know how to lead up to it. So I guess I'll just blurt it out. The thing is that that damned Molly Hart has been spreading a report about you."

"About *me?*" Robin felt chilled with fear.

"As nearly as I can make out she intimated to Hepsy that you had been, oh — you know — too intimate with her and all that, and now, she's well, she's the worse of it, she says."

Robin sat stunned. His face was white and his mouth at first felt too dry to speak. It seemed as though an intolerable weight had fallen upon him, crushing him. At last he said, "I want to tell you the whole truth of this, Tom, I hope I don't *have* to tell you I'm completely innocent. My problem has been to keep out of the girl's way. All she's told Hepsy was a lie of course, but how can we get people in general to believe that? Here are the facts."

He told Tom then all the story: of Molly's pathetic offerings of herself; of his own effort to be implacable and yet kind; of his anxiety even before Tom's confession for fear Alice might somehow get a distorted version of the situation for there had been that one sympathetic little forehead kiss which the squire had seen. He ended by stating his utter despair now over the present rumor, which was certainly the worst yet.

Tom looked him straight in the eye and held out his hand. "I'm Alice's brother," he said simply, "and I'll stand behind you."

Now a rumor such as this spreads slowly, for there are many degrees of credence ranging from "She's a hussy, and I don't believe a word of it," to "Well, after all he was right there in the house and so was she." The more genteel ladies over teacups mentioned it only by polite circumlocution if at all; the coarser ones gossiping comfortably in kitchens spoke first of how pale and how *thin* Molly was. Then without fail someone would quote, "There's always a lank before a bank." The laughter at this was likely to be a bit ribald especially if a younger matron, wide-eyed, inquired the meaning of the proverb. "Oh, a woman's likely to get thin sometimes before she gets fat," would be the reply amid more laughter. But there was in the end a gentler spirit prevailing about Molly. Poor soul, they all said, for while she would always be cared for, she could have small hope of marriage. And that young Adair, with his poems and stories and such, handsome as they come, and it was said heir to the old cousins' fortunes, and more than that, engaged to a beautiful girl like Alice Newcombe unless she threw him over, now, how would he ever think of marriage with the likes of Molly Hart? No, it was just a young man's folly and of course not the first one.

Meanwhile there were many threads weaving into the warp and woof of the Callaway days. The squire, with a smirk he tried to cover with a sanctimonious pursing of his lips, talked in low tones with George Hastings and in an almost sepulchral voice behind the counter told what he had seen with his own eyes in the Adair kitchen. George stared at him in amazement which turned quickly into complacence.

"By Jove!" he said. "By Jove! So this has been going on for some time!"

"Well, I am only telling you what I saw."

"And Molly was crying, you say?"

"Tears just streaming down her cheeks."

"What do you make of that, Squire?"

The squire gave a short laugh. "Now George, I'm an old bachelor. Your opinion might be nearer the truth. But I would just say on general principles that she must have been pretty upset over something in their relations, now wouldn't you?"

George hurried out of the store with his paper hoping to find a few cronies on the street corner to whom he could tell his latest tidbits. When he did find the others, however, Tom Newcombe was among them, which gave him pause. But not for long, as he was too eager to tell his news. He finally asked his question with an air of triumph.

"Well, Tom, what do you think now of your fine brother-in-law to be?"

"Just what I've always thought of him," Tom answered quietly.

"In spite of Molly's story?"

"Her story is a damned lie."

"Well what would make any girl start a rumor like that about herself?"

"I can think of a reason."

"Trying to trick him, huh? Well, I'll tell you something. It wasn't all on her side. The squire saw him *kiss* her, so what do you think of that?"

"I know all about it. If the squire gave you all the facts he would have told you Robin barely touched her forehead because he was sorry for her when she was upset and crying. It was the night after Miss Kitty had been so sick," he added.

George looked baffled for a moment, then gave utterance to his own proverb as he turned away. "Where there's so much smoke there's bound to be some fire. And after all it *was* a kiss!"

"Yes," said Tom dryly, "and I think we all know there are different kinds of kisses."

As he walked slowly home alone Tom's thoughts were troubled. He had absolutely no doubt of Robin's integrity, but that little devil, Molly, was a queer one and devious. She was evidently trying to scare Robin into marriage. Of all frightful things! Of course, he mused, time would prove the most serious aspect of her story false but even then, there would be a sort of scar on the public mind. "Of course, even so," and "There must have been something," and so on, as the gossips chattered. And Alice was involved in all this. That hurt, intolerably, for there had been a close and devoted relationship always between brother and sister. Robin had been the first man Tom had felt was worthy of her and he had rejoiced in the thought of their marriage, which would in truth give him a brother. Now, just as the wedding plans were taking definite shape, this, this dreadful thing, had come upon them.

He walked on past his own street, still thinking, until he found himself on the road that led to David Means's house on the edge of the woods. He looked ahead of him, startled, turned to go back and then changed his mind. Mr. Means was the one person to whom he could talk. Why not do it? He walked down the woodsy road and found the old gentleman on his front porch, looking haggard. When he saw Tom approaching he got up quickly to greet him.

"Tom! Why, my boy the Lord must have sent you! I haven't heard yet from Robin and I hesitated to call him. I'm not sure that he even knows about the scandal story yet. I heard it only today. I assume you know it or you wouldn't be here."

"It's nearly a week now since I first heard it but I just told Robin today. I felt he ought at least to know what was going on."

"Yes, he should. How did he take it?"

"Stunned."

"You believe in his innocence?"

"Absolutely. Don't you?"

"I do, indeed. First because of his character and second because I can't imagine a young man's getting himself into trouble over Molly's face."

"Or legs," Tom said gravely.

And then they both laughed, which relieved the tension. After that they settled to discuss the matter in full. There was, as Tom pointed out, the relatively near approach of the wedding. The bridal dress had been bought, Betsy, as bridesmaid, was going shopping for hers this week; there had been already discussions with the caterer.

"But all this could be adjusted. The worst thing is that Alice will have to be told by Robin himself. That will be terribly hard for both of them. A man just doesn't discuss this kind of thing with a girl."

David Means nodded and then said, "I sometimes wonder if our girls are not overprotected. Now Alice has good common sense and he won't need to spell this whole thing out for her. Do you think she'll trust him?"

"I'm sure of it."

"Well, that's the main thing but it's a nasty situation for them both when everything looked so rosy. What about your father? How will he take it?"

"I'm scared about that. He's been so friendly to Robin ever since he's gotten interested in the writing success. I heard him tell Alice once that he was glad she was going to marry such a 'pure, upright young man.' His words. Now I'm afraid this will send him into a frenzy. It's the sort of thing he feels strongly about. He's been talking a lot about the wedding too. Making jokes about 'giving her away,' and all of that." Tom drew a long sigh.

The two men talked and smoked until midnight, deciding again what small parts each could play in stemming the tide of gossip, in supporting Robin, in comforting Alice, then parted, each feeling the better of unburdening himself to the other.

But in the big Adair house there were lights burning long after midnight. Those in the sisters' rooms were out for, knowing nothing of the rumor that was rocking the town, they slept peacefully, conscious only of the pleasant aspects of their lives. In Robin's big room, however, there was no rest. He devised plan after plan, sometimes with his hands clenched, of telling the cousins all; of confronting Molly and demanding she tell the truth; of going to see the squire and overcoming him with his innocence and his wrath. But always he came back to the tragic, damning fact: a man was helpless before a girl's story; her oath, if it ever came to that, would stand in a court of law. Who ever said it was a man's world and he the strongest creature in it when a girl's lying word could destroy him?

And while Robin agonized in his despair Molly sat at the table in her own little room with an old volume open before her. Many of its pages were yellow and the binding worn from the use of two generations. It was known as *The Doctor Book* and Miss Jenny and Miss Kitty still consulted it when they suffered from minor ills. Molly had abstracted it carefully from the book shelves and once safely alone had turned the leaves to *Female Diseases*. It was upon *Pregnancy* that her eyes were now glued. As she carefully read *Symptoms,* she jotted down on bits of paper those she could make use of. Of course some did not apply to her and she hurried quickly over them. But *morning sickness!* She could pretend to Hepsy about that. *Sudden dislike to certain foods and unusual craving for others.* Now she could make a good deal out of *that* subject. She never did like cauliflower for one thing and she couldn't ever get enough of ice cream. That ought to be just right, one for the dislike and one for the craving, if she talked a good deal about each one.

At last she closed the book and put it under her pillow with the slips of paper marking it. Her face had a look of contentment as she put out the light and lay down in bed. She was smiling as she fell asleep. Her last thought was: *Some says this is an old trick but I'll bet it will catch him an' then it'll be me that will have him and not Alice.*

\*

And never were there brighter summer days than these, as though the elements were preparing for the wedding without a cloud. But sky-born clouds would have been as nothing compared to the dark disclosures and conjectures of the various townspeople as the ugly rumor spread and grew and lost nothing in the dissemination. Miss Jenny often eyed Robin anxiously at breakfast, one morning especially.

"Are you well, dear? You look pale to me. What about a small glass of boneset tea in the mornings? It's really an excellent tonic."

"No thank you, Cousin Jenny. The heat here is a little more than I like. I'm just a bit seedy but I'll soon pick up again." Then as a brilliant afterthought, "I have been lying awake sometimes."

Miss Kitty beamed. "But how very natural with all the wedding plans in your mind. Shall I tell him our idea for the honeymoon now, Sister?"

"I don't see why not. It might be better than a tonic. Sister Kitty and I would like to make it possible for you and Alice to go to Atlantic City then and stay at one of the very nicest hotels. Wouldn't you like that?"

"Like it?" Robin echoed, though his voice had a hollow sound. "I can't think of anything more wonderful, or more generous of you!"

"We'll discuss it later with Alice," Miss Kitty added archly, "and of course you can at any time you wish."

"Thank you so very much," Robin said, getting up from the table. "If I may call her now I'll see if we can get together this afternoon."

When Alice's voice came over the wire it sounded anxious.

"Is anything wrong, Robin? Tom acted very queer with me this morning."

"Don't worry," he said, "but I simply must talk to you today for I do have something on my mind. Could I pick you up for a drive about four?"

"Of course. Oh, Robin, is it something very bad?"

"Not if I'm with you. We'll straighten everything out."

"Robin?"

"Yes, dear."

"The ring looks more beautiful every day."

"So do you. I'll see you at four, then."

They drove in the Adair buggy once more around the lake and along the country road past Mr. Means's house to the woods. There Robin tied the horse. They sat on a bed of pine needles while Alice looked up at him inquiringly, all the more since he made no move to caress her.

"Darling," he said gravely, "have you heard any story, any rumor about me? Anything that would disturb you?"

"No," she said slowly, "except that Betsy asked me once if I still intended to marry you and I only laughed for I thought she was joking, and then Tom said this morning that if he were in my place he wouldn't go around talking to people until I'd first talked to you, so that troubled me, but that's all."

Robin looked at his hands as he sifted fragrant pine needles through his fingers.

"I have to do a hard thing, Alice. I have to repeat to you an ugly story that is being circulated about me. On Thanksgiving Day did you hear Molly Hart say anything that wasn't just *maidenly?*"

"I certainly did," Alice said angrily. "I heard her tell you to leave your door open. And then Grandfather told me later about — you know — the little kiss on her forehead."

"I'm glad you know that much. She's given me a lot of trouble. Twice she's come into my room and another time when your Grandfather was at the house, when we were snowed in, he intercepted her. But now she's told Hepsy and I guess it's all over town that I acted improperly with her and she's . . . she's . . . oh, how can I say this to you?"

"But I'm the very one you *can* talk to about it for I'm almost your wife."

"But she says she's in . . . in trouble because of me."

"I could choke her!" Alice burst out.

"You don't doubt me?"

Alice raised her sweet gray eyes to his. "I could never doubt you," she said simply.

And then at last their lips met. Before they left their pine-scented trysting place Alice looked up with a burst of joy.

"Why Robin, I've just thought. Don't you realize that if only we're patient for some weeks longer . . ." she blushed, "I don't know just how many, but if nothing happens to Molly your good name will be cleared. Don't you see? Her story will just fall apart. The only thing . . ."

"Yes, darling."

"I think we'll have to postpone the wedding. I *am* grieved about that but it isn't such a serious matter since we know it will still be coming soon. Do you agree?"

Robin nodded his head. "It's hard enough in all conscience for me to wait, but I don't want to marry you when there is the least cloud hanging over us — or me. I want it all sunshine and flowers, and we shouldn't have to wait too long for that. Why don't you talk it over with your mother, and with your Grandfather's amazing tact he might get some information out of Hepsy that would help us. Oh, I have one nice piece of news to cheer us up."

He told her then about the cousins' plans for their honeymoon at Atlantic City in one of the very best hotels. They started again, as though there had been no troubling intermission, to go over the happy wedding plans.

As they left, Robin said slowly, "I felt sure you wouldn't believe this awful story about me, but Molly has made it sound very true, I'm afraid."

Alice did not answer for a second, then she said softly, "I could never, never doubt you, Robin. Does Grandfather know?"

"Yes. He and Tom are both standing by me."

"Let's run in for a minute to the house as we pass it. We can find out if he knows anything new."

David Means was in his garden but came hastily to the porch as he saw the buggy stop. At the light on the two young faces his own drawn one relaxed.

"Come in to the porch and sit for a minute," he said, as he kissed his granddaughter. "I stand in need of the refreshment of true and faithful love. I mean the sight of it," he added. "You both look capable of beating the devil round a bush and pulling his tail for good measure."

"Grandfather, we're glad, Robin and I, that we can always count on you."

"Well, such as I am, I am completely at your service. How is the hussy, Molly Hart, behaving, Robin?"

"Just as usual, as far as I can see, except that she's jumpy and won't talk unless she's prodded."

"What about the old ladies? Has any gossip reached them?"

Robin knit his brows. "I can't understand it for they are having their *teas* as usual but I really don't think they've heard a thing. I don't know what to do about that situation."

David Means considered. "I think, Robin, no matter how unpleasant it may be, you should tell them the whole story. It's not right to keep it from them, for they are certainly bound to hear some time and then it would, in my opinion, look very bad for you that you had never taken them into your confidence. I would advise you to tell them at once."

Robin groaned. "I did want to wait until I told Alice, but now I've done so and she's been an angel. But telling the cousins is a different thing. This matter comes right into their own home and they are quite devoted to Molly."

"More so to you."

"Well, yes, perhaps, in a different way. But I would feel I was telling scandal to children!"

David smiled. "As to Kitty, yes, in a sense, but Jenny with all her innocent eyes has comprehended the ways of the world even though she hasn't experienced them. Jenny will grasp the situation. I'm not saying they won't be terribly upset, but at least they will know what's going on." He gave a short laugh. "There's an old wives' proverb, *More than one way to skin a cat; more than one way to catch a husband*. I have an idea Molly Hart has heard that, so I don't even trust the bare skeleton of her tale."

As the young people left, David gave Alice a convulsive little hug.

"I'm glad you have sense to stick to your young man. This trouble is bound to blow away. Just have patience. You're both young."

As they drove back Robin said, anxiously, "He didn't say a word about your father. I wonder if that's a bad omen."

"I can't understand it," Alice replied. "Father was growing very fond of you. Now, either that feeling is strong enough to counterbalance the rumor or else he's waiting to do something very drastic. I do feel a little frightened."

"Please don't be. That distresses me. We have each other, that's the main thing. Then we have your grandfather and Tom on our side and perhaps — your mother?"

"If she dares," Alice said slowly.

"Oh, is it like that?" Robin asked.

"I'm afraid so. My father is a very domineering person."

"So was mine," Robin said. Then he added, "I've often felt looking back that my mother had to yield unhappily on so many points to him. It makes me sad now to think of it. Alice?"

"Yes?"

"It will not be so with us when we are married. I have such tremendous love for you and such respect, that your wish, as they say, will always be my law."

She laid her head for a few moments against his shoulder and then said softly, "I'll try never to give you cause to regret that promise. Thank you, dear."

The matter of telling the unpleasant news to the cousins sent small tremors of fright over Robin's whole frame. "I'd rather take a flogging," he kept muttering to himself. However, he agreed with David Means that the thing ought to be done. The squire had been out several evenings and had assumed such a lugubrious air that Miss Jenny had asked him frequently if he were sick and given him a little packet of boneset leaves to take home with him for tea, assuring him that he would feel brighter at once.

"You do act worried, Squire."

"Only about the problems of my friends," he had replied.

So, Robin felt, his confession had better be made soon for it was evident the squire's powers of secrecy had limits. The very night after he and Alice had visited her grandfather, he waited until Molly had removed the after-dinner coffee cups, then closed the folding doors, and after clearing his throat, which *would* keep husky, he began.

"Dear Cousin Jenny and dear Cousin Kitty, I have something to tell you which I know will distress you and which is very hard for me to say . . ."

"You haven't broken off with Alice!" Miss Kitty quavered.

"No, *no!*" he said. "Oh, never that. But this trouble has to do with Molly Hart."

Miss Jenny looked sharply at him. "What was she doing in the hall the night I found her there with you?"

"That is part of the story. I want to be fair to Molly. I

don't think she ever knew a young man until I came here to live. Then as time went on, she . . . she thought she was in love with me and wanted me to love her in return, which of course I could not do. Several times she even came into my room and I finally put a lock on my door. I was very much troubled, but I didn't see any reason then for worrying you. But now it's gone further."

He swallowed painfully as he watched the two old ladies sitting quietly, their faces stricken, their hands folded in their laps.

"She has made up a story which she told Hepsy first and now it's all over town. She says I acted improperly with her and that now she is . . . well . . . pregnant."

"The little devil!" Miss Kitty said promptly.

Miss Jenny sat very still. "Have you taken pains to deny this story, Robin?"

"I didn't hear it myself until last week, then Alice's brother thought I should know. I was completely stunned, but he held out his hand and said he'd stand behind me. When I told Alice — and that was hard, to talk about such a thing to her — she said she trusted me completely, and so does Mr. Means. Those are the only people I've spoken to and in a sense I haven't denied the story for it seemed so incredible and those three thought so too."

"Dear boy," Miss Jenny said, "and so do we, don't we, Sister? But there's something wrong here about Molly Hart that we'll have to straighten out. A woman can talk to another woman of any age about matters that a man, especially a young one, can't. I will have a talk with Molly soon and find out what's behind all this. I think her imagination has just run wild and I may find some facts that can be quietly passed on to the town. The squire, for instance, has been throwing out broad hints about some threats hanging over us. Well, I think we can dispel those. And now, Robin, relax and forget the gossip. My advice would be to go on your way as usual. You know at our afternoon teas we have a good chance to counteract any unpleasant rumors."

"And we ought to tell you plainly, dear Robin," Miss Kitty put in, "that we, too, trust you completely."

"That goes without saying," Miss Jenny said. "The Adair men have all been *gentlemen* and so, of course, are you. I'm only sorry that such unpleasantness should have come to you under our own roof, as it were. But don't worry. This is a figment of the imagination and as such will all blow away. Good-night, dear boy."

Robin went to his room feeling as he used to after the strain of a hard school examination was over. At least the cousins seemed to hold no question in regard to him. What Miss Jenny would find out about Molly was another and very serious matter. Her face these days as she went about her work was pale and pinched; she did not glance at Robin as she served the meals, and answered the cousins briefly if at all. To Robin's relief, however, her body did not seem to be filling out in suggestive places.

The interview between Molly and Miss Jenny was inhibited in the extreme because of the latter's virginal delicacy on the one hand and the other's stubborn resistance to free communication on the other. It took place in the library behind closed doors and went in this wise:

"Molly, I wish to talk to you on a very serious subject."

"Yes'm."

"I have just heard that you have told a dreadful story about Mr. Robin which is not true."

"Who says it ain't?"

"Why, anybody would know it isn't true. He is not that kind of young man."

"Mebbe young men are all alike."

"No. Now Molly, for some reason you have made up this lie and told it and now it has spread through the town. What I want you to do is to start at once, *today,* to contradict it. Stop it, at once. That is my order."

Molly gave a short and unpleasant laugh.

"You might as well try to stop the wind from blowin' as to stop a story once it's got started in this town. Was this all, Miss Jenny? I'll be gettin' back to my work."

"But Molly . . . I . . . I . . . are you . . . I mean . . . you're not . . . you know . . . what you said you were . . . you simply *couldn't* be. You're no more that than I am . . . and it's a wicked thing to pretend . . ."

"Well," Molly said calmly, "I couldn't rightly say what condition other people might be in." And she turned around and left the room, with Miss Jenny gasping behind her.

When Robin asked about the interview, he found Miss Jenny near to tears as she spoke of it.

"I got *nowhere!* I can't even remember what little she did say. She was *evasive.* I wish I'd had David Means talk to her. He has a way of making people answer him. But I really thought this was a woman's business. Oh, Robin, I don't believe she will be of any help in denying the rumor.

Perhaps we'll just have to hold our heads high and go on as usual. The truth is bound to come to light."

Although it was against all her inherent modesty, Miss Jenny, after having David Means to dinner one night, asked him frankly what could be done to stop Molly's story. Robin had left the house in order to give them more freedom for discussion, and now David, serious for once, went over the whole matter, using the proper words without mincing them or the conditions to which they referred. At the end of the talk he shook his head.

"I'm afraid we've come out at the same door wherein we went," he said sadly. "Unless Molly herself contradicts the story I fear no one else can."

"Tell us more about Alice's reaction," Miss Kitty begged.

"True as steel, I'm glad to say. And so is Tom. They are both telling the young people the right way of it and Tom is adding some facts that I hope will be helpful. On the other hand George Hastings is doing his worst, of course. And girls," he said, using his name of long ago for them, "I do wish you would talk pretty straight to the squire and turn another pin in his nose if you can. He's in a position there to do either a lot of good or a lot of harm." He hesitated. "One thing I haven't told you."

"Tell us what it is," Miss Jenny said. "We're so troubled now, we can't be hurt much more."

"Well," David said slowly, "I put Hepsy on the carpet and told her if she wanted to keep her job she must tell me all she knew about Molly's story. She brought out the main facts that we've heard, then she added — this is what I hate to tell you — that Molly had confessed to having symptoms of pregnancy, morning sickness, for one, and *dis*like for certain foods, cauliflower, for instance . . ."

"Why, she *never* liked cauliflower," Miss Kitty said sharply, adding, "The very idea!"

"And she has a terrible craving for ice cream all the time . . ."

"Always had," Miss Kitty snapped.

"Well, that's good news. I wondered where that would leave us with the rumor if she *did* think she was developing symptoms. Of course Doc told me once that this so-called morning sickness business was largely in women's minds."

"And Mrs. Alder, our cleaning woman, told me she had heard the report and she had been noticing Molly carefully and didn't believe a word of it. David, I always feel better after talking with you."

"So do I," Miss Kitty echoed. "And we'll just go on our accustomed way?"

"Absolutely."

"Do you think if you talked to Molly yourself . . ." Miss Jenny hesitated.

"No, I have a feeling that would only make her more stubborn. I suppose she's silly enough to keep hoping still that Robin will look on her with favor?"

"Oh, I'm afraid so. I have caught her once or twice watching him with tears in her eyes."

"Poor kid," David said. "In spite of all the ghastly trouble she's caused I still feel sorry for her. Robin is so attractive, as we know, and being in the same house with him has evidently set Molly's emotions on the rampage." He drew a long sigh and added, "One good thing about age is that the emotions lie pretty dormant. As Mr. Robert Browning says,

> I've grown peaceful as old age tonight;
> I regret little, I would change still less.

So there you see there are advantages in getting old. At least we can watch young love like Robin's and Alice's without stirring up the fire."

"Oh, it's so lovely to think of them and their coming wedding. But how long will they have to wait?" Miss Jenny asked.

"I don't think *too* long. This story by its very nature will die away before too many weeks."

"Robin says he simply will not marry Alice when he is under a cloud."

"He's right. Neither would I. But let's keep our chins up, act as if we had never heard Molly's accusation and I think all will eventually be well. I wish," he added thoughtfully, "I knew what that confounded son-in-law of mine is up to. He's too quiet to suit me."

"Maybe he just trusts Robin as the rest of the family do."

"Hope so."

"And you think it's all right to keep on talking about the wedding to Robin?"

"Most certainly. It's the one bright spot on the horizon."

So, the weeks passed. It would be inaccurate to say that the rumor stopped entirely and tongues were stilled, but there was, as with other pieces of scandal, what David Means called a softening of the edges. For one thing Molly showed no outward suggestion of her story's truth. She had always been rather shapeless so the women, eyeing her, could come to no conclusion. She was pale, however, and had a strained and nervous look. Hepsy when pressed for information usually said, "She ain't happy, Molly ain't," and let her questioners make what they could of that.

So time went on, the June roses had never been so lovely and profuse, it was remarked; there was a tremendous Fourth of July celebration with a festival and some real fireworks; and after the concentration of all thoughts upon this occasion, men and women began gradually to slip into their old mental routines. They had been for many weeks preparing by thought and speech for a climax which did not occur and now it seemed relaxing to speak of the pleasure and small excitements of the celebration instead, and allow the scandal (if it *had* been a scandal) to drift into casual remarks. Even the squire in his stationer's shop found it difficult to fan the dying embers into a flame, the more so because he had been rather hurt by Miss Jenny's plain talk with him and also because he was a bit puzzled himself.

So this was the state of things in Callaway in early July when hollyhocks bloomed along the garden fences; when sweet peas filled the air with fragrance; when bees, laden with their sacrificial sweetness, added a soft languor to the sunny afternoons; and men and women went about their work as usual.

After dinner one night in the big Adair house, as Robin sat

with the cousins before the opened French windows in the front parlor, Miss Jenny waited until the last coffee cups had been removed and then, with a careful glance at the hall doors to be sure Molly was safely back in the kitchen, she began with a bright little air of excitement to speak.

"Robin dear, Sister and I have sometimes made joking remarks about this house being big enough for two families, but today we have been talking it over seriously. I'm sure your wedding need not be postponed too much longer. David, that is, Mr. Means, says the gossip has quite died down. Now I'm sure under the circumstances you haven't felt like looking for a place to live, and what Sister Kitty and I propose is this."

She stopped for breath and then went eagerly on. "We thought we could arrange a little apartment for you right here. We almost never use the library nor the back parlor and the bedroom above, just across from our rooms, is empty. There is an extra bath there already. You could be off to yourselves as much as you wish and entertain your young friends . . ."

"And Alice could redecorate the rooms as she liked. You see you would be alone and yet under our roof and we could see you at meals. Later, we know you'll want a house of your own but for a while just after you are married, do you think Alice would like this?"

"I think she would love it," Robin said, "and so would I. And it would settle so many problems that have been worrying us. But how can we ever thank you?"

"By staying on here for as long as you find it convenient."

"There's only one drawback. I suppose you know what I mean," he said slowly.

"But we've talked that all over too. You see if you were living here with Alice, with *your wife,* that would change everything. Molly would get used to the idea of it, seeing you together every day, and she would get over those feelings she had about you."

"She certainly knows even now, what *my* feelings are about her. But once I'm living here as a married man, as Alice's husband . . . upon my word you may be right! She might then sort of turn the romance around vicariously and really enjoy having us here."

A queer sound which might have been a cough but which sounded more like a sob came to them from the depths of the hall. They looked at each other, startled.

"Could that have been Molly?"

"Could she possibly have been listening?"

They whispered their questions anxiously.

Miss Jenny finally settled it. "Molly has her faults but I don't think eavesdropping is one of them. Well then, Robin dear, we'll consider the matter settled if Alice feels satisfied with the plans. If she decides to do some redecorating, she could begin any time. It might brighten her spirits while she's waiting for the wedding, and I imagine Molly would take a great interest in it."

There were still many details to talk over happily. Robin grew more and more enthusiastic and finally confessed that he had once told Alice of the cousins' comment that their house was large enough for two families, and that she had said then, "Oh, I wish it really could be!" So her response to the definite plan was certain. They all delayed bedtime. Robin called Alice and Mr. Means too, giving each a joyous if cryptic message. He insisted on escorting the old ladies out for a stroll on the long portico so they could see the golden moon rising over the meadow just beyond their wide property. But at last it seemed that all had been commented upon, all had been said, and with tender good-nights they all went upstairs to bed. There was no other movement anywhere else in the house. And if Molly had indeed heard the plans under discussion, if the strange sob had come from her heart, there was no sound now unless it was smothered in her pillow.

The lights went out, one by one through the town, the Old Girl had long, long since gone her stately way down the valley, the recent storm which had lashed the creek had grown calmer and the various travelers by the way had evidently reached their desired havens, and all was quiet.

The next morning Robin whistled blithely as he dressed. He rejoiced that the unpleasant surmises which had at first flooded the town had, according to Mr. Means' astute prophecy, indeed given place to new bits of local color and the general decision that Molly's story had been the figment of a girl's overwrought imagination. It would certainly be possible soon to have the wedding with no dark cloud hanging over it. Oh, the unutterable relief to his heart! And now, the plan for the apartment here in the house, close to the dear old cousins who loved Alice also so dearly, and yet not *too* close, always able to slip away to their own little nest furnished to their heart's desire and be alone — alone with each other! Oh, the bliss!

He was still whistling "I'll Come to You, My Love," as he came down the broad stairs but stopped suddenly at sight of Miss Jenny coming from the dining room with a frightened look on her face.

"What is it?" he asked anxiously.

"It's Molly. She's . . . she's *gone!* She hasn't made the breakfast. She hasn't even set the table . . ."

"Have you looked in her room?" Robin broke in.

"Oh, the first thing. There's no sign of her and nothing has been touched there."

"Did she take her clothes?"

"Just what she had on last night. Oh, Robin, I'm terrified."

"She's sure to turn up," he tried to answer bravely. "Would she be getting flowers in the garden?"

"No," called Miss Kitty, coming in through the kitchen. "She always brought fresh flowers in after she started the breakfast, but I've been talking just now with Charles and he says he hasn't seen a glint of her. Oh, Robin, what shall we do?"

"I'll tell you. First of all we'll get some breakfast. I can make coffee and scramble eggs and by the time we've eaten something I'll wager Molly will show up and tell us where she's been. Now, here I go to the kitchen. Could you both set the table and make toast? We'll have breakfast in a jiffy. Now, don't worry."

"Oh, you're such a comfort, Robin. I feel better already."

They were having their coffee, their scrambled eggs and toast and becoming cheered up sufficiently to suggest various explanations of Molly's disappearance, when a knock came on the French doors on the portico.

"I'll go," Robin said, trying to conceal a tremor of the lips.

When he opened it David Means took him firmly by the arm and said gently, "Hold steady, Robin. I'm afraid it's bad news. This," as he indicated a large red-faced man behind him, "is Officer Banks, who insisted on coming out with me."

"Well," said the officer in a loud voice, "when it comes to this kind of thing, the law has to be what help it can, I'd say."

"Where are the ladies?" David went on as though he had not heard the policeman's remark.

"At their breakfast."

"I'm glad they've had their morning coffee. Maybe I could just go in to talk to them in the dining room."

But Miss Jenny was already almost beside them, with Miss Kitty following.

"David, what is it? What's happened to Molly? She didn't get our breakfast. She isn't here anywhere. What are you keeping from us? Tell us the truth. We must know where she is and go after her."

David Means started to speak and could only push them down to the little sofa behind him. "Dear old friends . . ." he began, and stopped.

Officer Banks spoke at once. "They've got to know. There ain't any way of breakin' news like this. The plain fact is your girl Molly she's done away with herself. Some boys were fishin' early this morning an' they found her clothes, shoes an' all, under the willow branches by the crick an' I guess that just about tells the story."

"Get the smelling-salts for them, Robin," David said. "I've brought some brandy."

He poured a vial for each of them and made them drink it. Robin brought the volatile and still neither of them spoke.

"Could you go back to your duties now, Officer, and leave the ladies to me?" David Means said. "This is a family sorrow and I am close to them."

"There are a few questions I have to ask," the officer said, as though fearful of losing some of his status. "Now, Miss Jenny, just how did Molly seem last night?"

"As usual," she said in a husky voice.

"And when was the last you saw her?"

"At nine o'clock when she finished her work."

"Did she go at once to her room?"

"I assume so. That was her custom."

"Had she seemed depressed before this time?"

"Not especially."

The officer turned to look at Robin who, with a face as white as chalk, had sunk into the chair behind him.

"Of course there'll be an inquest after the body's found an' then there will be more personal questions. They're draggin' for the body now an' . . ."

David Means grabbed the officer's arm. "We know you have to do your duty but could you please go on now and leave the ladies alone? They've had a great shock and they aren't strong. Let them rest a little and adjust to this sad news. Thank you," he added, as he propelled Banks out of the door. "Thank you very much. We'll call on you if we need you."

When the astonished officer had left, David locked the French doors and then sank down also. The four stricken faces looked at each other.

"I wish I could cry," Miss Kitty quavered at last. "I cried when Tommy our cat died and . . . and about other things, but somehow I can't cry about Molly. It's too heartbreaking. I can't remember when anyone else in town ever was a . . . I mean ever committed . . ."

"Robin," David Means spoke quickly, "can you heat up some more coffee for the ladies and if there's any whiskey in the house . . ."

"There is."

"Bring a stiff one for me and yourself too. We'll have to get pulled together."

When Robin came back with a tray, the cups and glasses jostled each other a bit from his unsteady hands, but when he set them down at last it was he who spoke first.

"I think," he said, "that because of this dreadful tragedy it is due you that I should tell you again that I am completely innocent of any harm in any way to Molly. She had a most unfortunate feeling for me, as you know, which I could not of course return and she was very unhappy."

There was silence until David said slowly, "I think you must realize that in the opinion of the town the matter of unrequited love would not be enough to make Molly take her life. There was, you know, more to her story than that."

Robin looked stunned. "And in your opinion?" he asked huskily.

David gave the ghost of a smile. "Oh, no," he said. "My confidence once given, remains. I am only shocked and deeply distressed as we all are, and I was merely pointing out that we must be prepared for what will be in the minds of the town."

Miss Jenny's head bowed suddenly on her hand. "Poor Molly!" she murmured. "Oh, poor Molly. I think we should have talked to her after we knew her feelings. We might have comforted her and advised her. I really feel a little faint . . . if one of you could help me up to my room . . ."

"I'll go too. My head swims," Miss Kitty added.

The men were at once on their feet, David by Miss Jenny's side and Robin with Miss Kitty. They were both pale and cold and trembling.

"I'll get Doc at once," David said, when they had seen the old ladies safely in bed under warm coverlets.

"No, we won't undress," Miss Kitty had announced. "We might still have to answer questions. Oh, *poor* Molly!"

The doctor came at once and checked them carefully. "They are weak. They must rest, and they will need a helper at once. This is a bad business."

"I'll call Hepsy. She has a flock of relatives. She'll be so broken up that some active part in the matter will be good for her," David said.

Hepsy when called was near hysteria but was somewhat

prepared, having read of coming disaster in her tea leaves. She had a cousin who she was sure would come at once. Her name was Pearl. And she hoped now people in town would not blame Molly for making up her story. If it hadn't been true why would she have drownded herself? And she, Hepsy, had always suspected something like this would happen and she could tell them a few things yet if she was . . .

David Means told her to get Pearl there as fast as possible and hung up the receiver. He came back to Robin with a drawn face. "I'm afraid, my boy, we will be in for a bad time. Worse than before. This floors even me. You can see, yourself, how it looks on the face of it. Molly has always been a queer girl, this business of love was new to her and hit her hard. I can see how she actually with her mentality would choose death. But the other hint she threw out which the town had decided was a piece of imagination will now seem to be substantiated by what has happened. At the moment I can't see how we can combat it. I do grieve for all concerned and certainly not least for you. Of course," he added, "when the body is recovered . . ."

Robin's voice was unsteady. "What about Alice? What can I say? Will she still believe me after this? I think it might be better for her if I left town."

"No," David said strongly. "You know the saying, 'He's armed without who's innocent within.' You can't leave the old ladies to bear this alone. Your place is here. As to Alice, the thing that concerns me most is her father. He's been entirely too quiet, as though he were really waiting for something to *break*. Well, it's broken all right and what he may do I wouldn't hazard a guess."

"He couldn't sway Alice against me?" Robin asked with something like terror in his voice.

"I'm sure he couldn't. But Robin, this is no time to gloss over facts. They must be looked in the face and these are very damning. The whole town will react, I fear, just as I've told you Hepsy did. I think, though, hard as it will be, you'll have to go on your way as usual and bear the blame you don't deserve."

"I don't see how even you can believe in me after this."

"I was a young man once and I know what difficulty beset me at one time. Besides, I like the straight look of your eyes, so you needn't worry about me, but the trouble is there is nothing really we can say to the town, except that it was a sad accident to a poor, foolish, love-sick girl. *I* can say that but you may just have to speak as the spirit moves you at the time."

"If I could only talk to Alice, but it shouldn't be on the telephone. I think I'll stop in this evening and try to see her."

"Good idea. Meanwhile I'm weak as a cat for I've had no breakfast. Suppose we have some and then both stay around today to meet any questioners. God save us from the squire! It's a wonder he hasn't been here already."

He came soon after and pointing a long, bony finger at Robin, hissed, "You *murderer!*"

"That'll do, Squire," said David Means, "he's no more murderer than you or I. What poor Molly did, she did of her own accord. Come on out and have some breakfast with us. The ladies are resting."

After several cups of coffee with food to go with them, the squire who, as a solitary bachelor, ate scantily, began to view the tragedy with more calmness and even discussed with the others the best way to meet the flood of distressed comments and questions.

"I believe you, Squire, are the best fitted to handle many of these, if you will. Your store is always a place where neighbors gather. Now, if you could say that you knew for a fact that Robin here had tried to be sympathetic with Molly — I think you know what I mean — and also that you have my word that when I stayed here once over night I saw with my own eyes how he had to fend her off. These things you could say to explain how a young girl of low mentality could, when she saw there was no hope for her, drown herself for love. It's happened before in the world. I feel you have a duty in this, Squire."

The squire metaphorically licked his lips. "Well, I'm not one to shirk my duty."

"I'll speak in much the same vein, but I think it will be best for Robin to say as little as possible."

So it was planned. The squire left almost at once to be early on hand to dispense his information. The old ladies were asleep from exhaustion, so David and Robin sat in the big front parlor and received the men from the local paper, who looked with rather knowing and piercing eyes at Robin.

"Thank goodness you were here, Mr. Means," he said when they left. "I'm sure I looked guilty enough to make them write anything about me."

There were many callers: old friends filled with real sympathy, and gossips and busybodies eager to glean what lugubrious bits they could. David handled them all with tact and firmness. At four the doctor returned, stated flatly that the shock had been hard on the hearts of both old ladies and ordered bed rest for the following day also. And soon after his departure Pearl, Hepsy's cousin, arrived and took calm possession of everything. She was a good-looking woman of middle age and her aplomb was superb. She visited Miss Jenny and Miss Kitty and they felt at once that they were in capable hands.

"Now, don't you worry about a thing," she assured them. "I'll serve you a nice little supper up here and I'll make it early, for Mr. Means says you haven't had any lunch. I'll fix your pillows a bit now and get you a light blanket for over your feet. These nights get cool."

As she talked she straightened the pillows, smoothed the sheets, patted the thin old shoulders gently and in a very short time was back with supper trays, the delicacy of which viands Molly could never have achieved.

"You see I've been workin' in a tearoom an' it closed down, so it's providential you might say that I was free to come."

When bedtime arrived and the men well served with dinner, the ladies were settled for the night with a pleased astonishment filling their minds. Molly had done her work faithfully, obeyed orders dutifully, but anything like affection had never showed through her stolid exterior. Now, with something bordering on disbelief they had found themselves deftly disrobed and finally tucked between the sheets like children. Pearl could not actually be said to caress them but there was a look of tenderness in her eyes and a gentle touch to her hands that soothed and comforted the two stricken old hearts.

"Now, don't you worry about a thing," Pearl admonished them as she left. "I'll be right across the hall if you need me and Mr. Robin and Mr. Means will both be here. Well, goodnight, dearies."

But while Miss Jenny and Miss Kitty were finding a small surprised tranquillity to ease the pain of the day's happening, Robin was utterly sick at heart. He had gone right after dinner to the Newcombe home, found the door closed and rung the bell. Mr. Newcombe himself had appeared.

"Good evening, sir," Robin had said politely. "I came to speak to Alice if she is in."

"She is not," Newcombe said shortly, "and will never be again — to you."

Robin looked at him, too stunned to answer.

"I am surprised," Newcombe went on, "that you had the outrageous lack of shame to come here to see her after the terrible tragedy in which you are involved."

Robin's strong chin set. "I am not involved in that tragedy, sir."

"How do you make that out?"

"I could not help it if Molly fancied herself in love with me. I kept out of her way as best I could. Surely you of all people should realize I would be true to the girl I love."

"And what about the rest of Molly's story? The part that

evidently made her take her life? How can you explain that?"

Robin looked straight into his eyes. "I can't," he said.

"Well then. You'd better forget my daughter completely."

"*Forget* her? I'm going to marry her."

"Not now, you're not. As soon as we heard the shocking, the awful news, I made her and her mother pack their clothes and leave for Atlantic City. Tom has a vacation coming up so he will join them. I don't like to have them there alone."

"But did Alice leave no note . . . no message for me?"

"Why should she after what has happened? I tell you there will now be no communication whatever between you. My instinct about you was right in the first place. Good evening, Mr. Adair."

When Robin reached the stone house again where Mr. Means was waiting his legs were trembling under him. He sank down opposite the older man as though all strength had left him. For a long minute he could not speak and his face was ghastly white.

"Bear up, my boy," David said. "Hold steady. This has been a dreadful day and you've been brave. Don't break now."

And then Robin's voice came brokenly. "Alice has gone away with her mother and left no message for me."

## Chapter Eight

THE CANODOQUINNETT, which as a rule quietly bathed the edge of Callaway and gave young lovers the chance for romantic canoe rides, had one well known idiosyncrasy. Perhaps because it emptied into the great river not too much farther down, perhaps because its bed had a faint slope in that direction, or perhaps because its pebbly bottom created a certain accelerant, no one knew. But the fact was, that while ordinarily the creek ran its placid way, a violent rain storm sent it churning a swift and white capped torrent toward the river.

For this reason many an overturned canoe had never been recovered, many a nice piece of wearing apparel such as a fancy scarf or cape, which should have been salvaged when the storm subsided, was lost forever; but, most tragic of all, over the many years the bodies of those who, feeling life insupportable, had tried to find surcease from their woes in the waters of the familiar creek, had never, never been found again.

*

The blithe, bright day, which had begun with Robin's whistling did not have a repetition on the following one. As the hours passed, the men with their grim faces and grappling hooks who were still at their heavy task in the creek, looked at the pouring rain, the heavy skies and the sudden roiling waters around them and cursed the weather. By late afternoon they had to get themselves and their boats to the bank as best they could. Their rough faces were drawn.

"She's gone by now," one said.

"When the crick's quietened down we might try near the river."

"It's worse there. You mind Whitey Newland? It's a mercy we didn't all get swept out the river, tryin' to get him."

"We've done our best. But who'll tell the old ladies?"

"Mebbe Mr. Means."

"Well, young Adair has got his desserts all right. I doubt he'll have a thorny bed to sleep on now. Do you think the Newcombe girl will still marry him?"

"I heard she and her mother left town as soon as they heard the news."

"We'd better be gettin' to the fire. I'm soaked to the skin an' cold for sure. Who'll go up to the Adair house?"

"Mr. Means will know without much tellin'. He's lived here long enough. You know I still keep thinkin' of that girl in the water, that is. She wasn't much to look at but still an' all she was young."

They dispersed, heavy-hearted, one neighbor volunteering to speak to David Means. He had been correct in his surmise. David needed little information. He had known since mid-afternoon what the report would be. He turned from the door, shutting the rain and darkness out, and came back to the old ladies, now down stairs, and Robin sitting white and strained in the parlor. As the door closed a flash of lightning came, followed by a violent clap of thunder that seemed to shake the house.

"These summer storms," David tried to say calmly, "are the worst of the year. I suppose it's due to the extreme heat and then sudden currents of cooler air. But I'm no meteorologist. What's your idea, Robin?"

"They terrify me. We don't have them in England, you know. I still shake like a child over sudden thunder. I wonder if I'll ever get over it. Oh, here comes Pearl."

It was indeed Pearl pushing a tea cart from which sweet odors floated. The old ladies cheered up at once as they always did at the sight of food.

"I just says to myself," Pearl went on, "what they all need right now is a cup of tea and hot muffins. Mr. Robin, if you'll just help me pass."

Robin jumped from his chair with relief as David Means said, "Pearl, you are inspired."

In a twinkling small tables appeared, and cups of tea along with plates of hot buttered muffins and marmalade were circulated freely. And with it all, color returned a little to blanched cheeks, and a bit more strength to faint voices. And when he felt they could stand it, David spoke very gently of the swiftness of the *Canodoquinnett* in a storm and of how it bore all its burdens with it away to the great river beyond. No one spoke for some time. Robin sat with his hand over his eyes; Miss Jenny held her beautiful white head erect, glancing often as though for strength at David, who in their youth had been in love with her. It was Miss Kitty who finally with a child's naive practicality voiced what was in all their minds.

"If that's the way it is," she said, "we'll be spared a funeral. I've kept thinking that I couldn't bear that. And now the Lord's just taken it out of our hands, as it were. It's like the hymn says, he moves in a mysterious way . . . what's that verse, David?"

David quoted:

> God moves in a mysterious way
> His wonders to perform;
> He plants his footsteps in the sea
> And rides upon the storm.

"Yes, that's it. The storm. That was what saved us. Are you there, Pearl?"

"Yes, Miss Kitty."

"I think I'll have another cup of tea and a muffin. I do feel stronger since the food." She still kept saying as she drank her tea, "The storm. That's what did it. The storm."

Of them all, Robin looked the whitest. He had tried to get in touch with Tom both directly and through Betsy but the results were not encouraging. If Betsy knew where the Newcombes were staying she did not tell. Finally Robin went up to his room, more shaken and despairing than he had ever been in his life. With the honesty that was inherent in his nature he realized that the shock of Molly's death and its cause would certainly prevent Alice from wanting to see him just then. He couldn't blame her. He could think of no way in which he was to blame, but all the same he had within him a sad, almost agonized feeling of guilt when he thought of the burden the waters bore and the stress of the emotion in poor Molly's breast. Yet Alice could have left him a message. She must have known how his own heart was aching.

He paced back and forth as he had done the night he had first known of his love. He pondered upon what his course of action should be. Here he must be guided by Mr. Means, but even so he was himself a man and must exert his own powers of judgment. The ghastly, damning fact in connection with Molly's death was that no one would believe now in his innocence. The vague story she had circulated could now, with no inquest possible, never be disproved. He would in the old phrase always be "under a cloud." And Alice? With all her faith in him, she was a pure and sensitive girl, he was a young and virile man, how would even her faithful heart construe this last tragic testimony against him? But she could have at least left a message, he said aloud, once again.

"Mr. Robin, sir," came in Pearl's voice from the stairway, "dinner is served."

Something strange happened during the meal. The old ladies brightened noticeably, and David Means also seemed to throw off the heavy shadow and converse as usual. Even

Robin, the saddest of all, felt a stirring of hope, for Pearl in her own fashion was doing her best to lift the heaviness. While Molly's cooking had been excellent in its plain way, Pearl's had a touch of surprise to the palate which amounted almost to ambrosia. Before the dinner had ended David and the cousins had all begun to talk in normal tones and Robin himself, amazed that anything as mundane as food could affect his spirits, had begun to have a small feeling of relief.

David Means stayed that night after a talk with both Hepsy and Pearl. The latter was delighted with her new place and would definitely remain to look after things and cheer up the old ladies though it was a sad business and all. Hepsy was depressed but cheered a little as she found Pearl would stay on. "She's good company to walk out with," Hepsy said, "though I'll be missin' Molly, an' I can tell you the town's pretty bitter about the whole thing. You'd ought to hear George Hastings. He says he wishes they still tarred and feathered people. He'd certainly help with Mr. Robin."

Mr. Means gave a few curt directions and hung up. But he was alarmed none the less. It was agreed, however, between him and Robin that they must pursue the usual course of their days. This could now be more easily carried out when Pearl was there to look after the old ladies. But the attitude of the town expressed itself promptly and was hard to bear. For once the squire's pronouncements, delivered sotto voce to make them sound more impressive, were accepted eagerly. There were no disclaimers or attempts at argument. To all and sundry the facts themselves seemed to shout out louder than any explanation of them. Molly had been a long familiar figure in the town. She belonged to it. Robin was once again a stranger, an object first of suspicion, and now of mistrust and evil-doing leading to a tragedy. What else could anyone say or think?

Mr. Means's efforts at palliation were in vain; his discourse with his son-in-law was worse than useless for it had led to angry words on both sides and thus accomplished nothing. As to Robin himself, he went back and forth to the office, pale and silent and most of those he met passed him by with the merest nod or no sign at all. "I'm being sent to Coventry, all right," he often thought. "But how long can I stand it?"

All this would have meant relatively little to him if he had only had some sort of contact with Alice. He had begun with Betsy, begging her help with all his powers of persuasion. She surely knew where Tom was staying. *Wouldn't* she tell him? He was going mad with the silence. This was not like Alice. She had trusted him. But Betsy was gently obdurate. She and Tom had had a quarrel before he left. She didn't know where he was. Under the circumstances, of course she wasn't writing to Alice. She was sorry, but she couldn't help Robin. He would just have to wait.

"For how long?" he burst out.

"I wouldn't know. Tom has his vacation but the others might stay longer."

"Make it up with Tom, Betsy. Don't let anything come between you."

Betsy gave her head a little toss. "I don't think I'm like your song, 'Whistle and I'll Come to You.' I think he'll have to come to me, if he wants me. Sorry, Robin."

He left her uneasily, for he happened to know that Tom and Betsy were practically engaged. Could his own trouble have in any way caused their quarrel? But in any case why, why had he heard neither from Tom nor Alice?

There was another reason the Callaway men and women felt bitter, though they would never have recognized it, nor admitted it to themselves. They felt frustrated because there could *be* no funeral. For Callaway loved these lugubrious occasions. Not that they did not grieve, for often their sorrow even for old neighbors was very deep. It was because such times gave them a chance for normal expression of their own sadness and griefs which usually were kept deeply hidden. Many a woman came home from a funeral relieved of a burden she felt she could not go on carrying. "Earth has no sorrow that heaven cannot heal," she would sing as she prepared the evening meal.

Now there would be no funeral, and the thought of the swift waters only made the inner troubles seem more acute.

There was another form of disappointment for the women. At the time of a funeral there was intensive baking and cooking in many, many homes in the town. These viands were carried with loving sympathy to the bereaved family, just as black veils and skirts were carefully pressed in case extra articles of clothing were needed. All of this, of course, was discussed later in various kitchens.

"Sadie wore my veil. I was glad I'd taken it."

"I made the big chocolate layer cake Jake was always so fond of."

"I took sweet rolls. I thought they could have them with tea when they got back from the cemetery."

"Yes, it was a sad Providence."

Even the men of what might be called Callaway's middle class, who did not often have a chance to wear their best suits, felt an inch higher as they dressed carefully to do honor to a fellow workman.

All of this, while unknown to the various citizens themselves, and certainly to Robin, yet formed a part of the basis of frustration, unrecognized but true, for the cool nods or averted faces on the people he passed on the street.

After a week and further discussion with David Means and the cousins who now knew all the sad facts, David made a list under their direction of the hotels at which the New-combes might be.

"They would surely stay at a hotel on the boardwalk," Miss Jenny was positive.

"I don't know," David Means said thoughtfully. "New-combe holds the purse strings pretty tight. However, just now, under the circumstances, he might let himself go a little."

So the names of the great hotels were set down, along with some smaller ones where there would not be an ocean view but which might have a little gayety and elegance. The plan as Robin had devised it was for him to write to all these hotels in the hope that at one of them a letter might get through to Alice.

"I'm afraid," he repeated mournfully now, "it's still like hunting for a needle in a hay stack. There are so very many more hotels than we can possibly list."

"I'll try a few wires on my own," David said.

"And send some from us," Jenny put in quickly. "I never thought of that."

The letters and telegrams were dispatched; four hearts waited, trembling with hope. In spite of Pearl's superlative cooking Robin found at last he could not eat. There was a faint, very faint, relaxation in the dark mood of the town. At least the young people now spoke to him, but the dark and awful fact, of course, was unchanged, like a wall surrounding him. The little rushing creek had done its worst. Now all the townspeople could say was, "Poor, poor Molly!"

When two weeks had passed without any response from Alice, and with Mr. Newcombe and Betsy still in their different ways obdurate, Robin decided he could bear it no longer. Mr. Means counseled him to stay on, thinking not of himself but of the cousins, and also, too, of his reputation, which would definitely suffer if he left town. With it all, Robin felt the anguish of hope deferred, of downright fear for the loss of his love and the slow eroding of his self-respect which the town's attitude caused. At last he made a decision to which David and the cousins, looking at his thin white face, agreed. He would wait two more weeks hoping for news and by then if he had heard nothing, he himself would take a vacation. "He might even take Sister and me to Atlantic City, which would make it seem quite regular," Miss Jenny said, "for we usually go once a year and we certainly need a change now."

So it was arranged and the drowsy mid-summer days passed, as the first week and then the second saw the garden filled with mixed bloom and the town settling a little into the even tenor of its ways. On his day off Robin went out, heavy-hearted, to sit on the stone bench among the flowers.

Everything reminded him of Alice. It was right here, with the roses blooming then, that he had first talked alone with her and planned for their first real meeting. He sank forward, his head in his hands.

He did not hear light, running footsteps now through the soft grass. He heard nothing until her voice. He sprang to his feet then as though in a dream. But Alice herself stood there, her face wet with tears, her hands outstretched.

> I'll come to you, my lad!
> Oh, my love, I'll come to you.

There was so much to tell as they sat in each other's arms amongst the flowers. "Of course I'm nothing like Elizabeth Barrett, but really my father acted just like hers. We went to Atlantic City but only for a night and then Mother and I went on to my aunt's in Philadelphia where I was practically *immured*. She's even worse than Father. I couldn't get a letter posted! I couldn't use the phone, and poor Tom thought all the time we were in touch with you. When we got back today my mother really asserted herself for the first time! She was *wonderful* and Tom was furious. So Father actually seemed ashamed. From now on we ought to have no trouble. Oh Robin!" And they held each other close again.

One thing they agreed upon. They had waited long enough. They would get married soon. "Before anything more could possibly befall us," Alice said.

"Nothing will," Robin said, strong now in his joy. "I believe nothing but the most wonderful things will happen."

"We could just go quietly to the minister's. Grandfather would come and the cousins, and now my mother would, and of course Tom."

"What's up between him and Betsy?"

"I'm proud of him. He stuck up for you and for me. But they'll get everything smoothed out."

"And we'll have our little apartment here! And the woman Hepsy sent is a jewel."

"Oh Robin! I can hardly believe it! Even the sadness over poor Molly seems now to fade away. And you must always remember you didn't even have to whistle to make me come."

They could hardly leave the sunshine and the flowers with their own bliss touching it all, but they must go at last to tell the news to the old ladies, and call Mr. Means to come out at once if he could. Then there were tearful explanations and occasional laughter and great joy.

It was decided after the first happy day of unbelieving that the marriage should be delayed for at least a short time further, then the young couple with their closest relatives and friends could go quietly to the church for an evening ceremony, after which Charles could drive them to the junction to catch the train for the east where they would arrive at last for the honeymoon. Robin suggested strongly that this should all take place at once, but Mrs. Newcombe, who had come to assist with the plans, took charge with a firmness new to her, as though at long last she had risen to her rights as a woman and meant to keep them.

"You see, Robin," she explained, "the neighbors say the scandal is not talked about so much now, and if we delay just a little longer it will be all the better. Then, although it will be a very small wedding, Alice will want to have her wedding gown fitted and pressed again and she hadn't gotten her veil before nor all her trousseau so she ought to have the pleasure of having everything just right after all she's gone through, don't you see, Robin?"

He capitulated at once with a long look into Alice's eyes.

"We'll start things moving right away," Mrs. Newcombe went on. "I'll never forgive myself for giving in the way I did. I thought it was a wife's duty, but now I know better. You might say all at once I've got the bit in my own teeth and I'm going to keep it there. So let's go ahead with the plans. And I have a feeling Alice's father may fall in with them. He's had a big shock and it's done him good!"

"We would want to have a little collation for the guests here after the wedding," Miss Jenny said.

"Oh, by all means," echoed Miss Kitty. "I've just dreamed of a bridal reception."

"This will have to be rather quiet due to the circumstances, but the very fact that the young people are being married at all will make a slight change in the town's attitude, I think," David Means said. "So by all means have a little party but not too gay a one."

When Pearl heard of the coming nuptials and the "collation" afterwards, she rose to the idea as a trout to the fly. This was indeed her element and all could be left to her.

A caterer? Nonsense. Hepsy could help well enough if

she'd do it and it was Pearl's opinion that if anything like this was afoot she would stop mooning around and be her old self.

Other arrangements fell as smoothly into shape. Betsy, now completely happy again with Tom, got her bridesmaid dress and was full of plans for decorating the church and including a few more of the young folks whom Alice in her present bemused state had not remembered. The squire had news to tell to all and sundry and made many trips to the stone house to see if he could "be of service." The town's attitude gradually swung through condemnation to consideration to curiosity. When it reached a high point of the latter something very like romance began to drift in. There was to be a wedding after all.

There came a day at last, a never-to-be-forgotten day, a beautiful bright day, warm, sweet-scented with musk and stocks and some ever-blooming roses, when all was in readiness for the great occasion near at hand. The minister and organist knew their roles. At the Newcombes' the wedding dress and veil lay in Alice's room like a cloud dropped from heaven, with her going-away dress and trousseau bag at the stone house from which she would leave after the reception; the gowns of the other ladies, Miss Jenny, Miss Kitty and Mrs. Newcombe, were hung in elegant grandeur in their respective closets. Even the men had indulged in new suits — Robin, of course, but also David Means, and Mr. Newcombe, who in his present new and chastened state of grace was going to give Alice away. Most surprising of all was the squire, who upon learning he was to escort Miss Kitty up the aisle, threw economy to the winds and purchased a fine black, which with difficulty he kept from showing to all customers.

So, what with one detail and another, both large and small, all seemed in order. Sustained by one of Pearl's bountiful breakfasts, Miss Jenny decided one morning to repair to her room to tidy up her bureau drawers.

"And Sister Kitty," she called, "I would advise you to do likewise. You know at the reception" (a word they both rolled sweetly upon the tongue) "even though it's a small one, the ladies will come up here to leave their scarfs and boas and you can't tell who is going to peep into the dresser. Women are like that. So, I'm starting right now on mine, and I can finish after lunch."

She drew a chair before her bureau and very methodically began to sort the contents of the upper drawer: all the gloves were piled neatly at one side; the scarfs and oddments on the other. She had at last arranged the boxes of hairpins and jewelry, and was about to begin upon her handkerchief case of *mouchoirs,* as she preferred to call them, when she heard the arrival of the postman. Since letters pertaining to the wedding came constantly she left her work and went down to meet him. Miss Kitty was still in her room and Robin could be seen coming up the road. The postman laid one letter conspicuously on top of the others and, looking decidedly strange, left quickly.

Miss Jenny glanced at the handwriting and the name and address on the corner of the envelope, then she moved slowly back to a chair, sank down as though her legs were too weak to hold her and, without calling her sister, opened the letter. This is what she read:

Dear Miss Jenny and Dear Miss Kitty: I take my pen in hand to let you know I am well and hope you are enjoying the same great blessing, health that's the way my grand-father always begun a letter when he was alive but now I'm going straight on with what I want to say special. I have to tell you I never got drowned at all but it's awful hard to explain to you being maiden ladies how it was with me. I just loved Mr. Robin in a way you couldn't never understand and I can't put it delicate. I was beside myself wanting him to love me like I couldn't just tell you and he wouldn't do it. And I'd about decided to thole it as best I could when I heard you all talking one night about him and Miss Alice coming out to live with you when they was married and it put me clean crazy to think of watching them there together all the time day and nights too and I knowed I'd ruther die. So I never stopped to think. I just run out when you was all asleep to the Crick and stripped off my clothes and laid them under the willow and started into the water thinking how I'd just die quick and easy and the aching in my heart would be over. But I forgot the Crick is only deep in the middle and by the time I got to where the water was clean over my head I was scared then and I didn't want to die but I couldn't swim and I couldn't get back or forrards.

Miss Jenny put the letter down at this point to wipe her eyes. Then began again to read.

All I could do was dog-paddle and I don't know yet how I done it but I finally got to where I could touch bottom and come out right at old Missus Derby's shack, she they call the witch for she goes round selling yarbs and I knocked on her door and I was shivering and crying and naket as a jay. But she come and took me in and wrapped me up in old blankets and was good to me. I told her I couldn't stand it to go back to Callaway after all I'd done for it was me took the tacks out of the carpet and put the white stuff on the sassafras and made the noises and if I die I'm feared I'll go to hell for it. I never wanted to hurt you ladies but just to make you think Mr. Robin had done it and then I'd stand up for him and mebbe he'd love me. Anyway Missus Derby give me old clothes next morning and lent me money for she's got a sockful and showed me a woods path to the junction and so I'm here in the city at an aunt of Hepsy's but she won't tell. She needs help so I'll stay a while even if it ain't like being with you. I hope you can forgive me and pray for me and I thank you for all your kindness

from yours truly, Molly

P.S. I've put off writing this for it's been so hard to say.

Miss Jenny sat still a long minute, then, waving the letter in her hand, she went into the hall calling, "Sister Kitty! Oh Robin! Oh Sister Kitty!" For Robin had just entered for his early lunch.

The two came hurrying, with fright on their faces. When they reached Miss Jenny she couldn't speak, only cried and laughed hysterically and held out the letter.

There was tremendous amazement and rejoicing. "First of all," Miss Jenny kept saying, "because Molly is alive and well. Sister Kitty and I felt the . . . the tragedy more than any one ever knew. And now there is *no* tragedy! And

Robin the wedding can be . . . oh do call Alice at once."

"I'll do better," Robin burst out. "I'll go to see her to tell her in person. And I think Mr. Means should see the letter. We want the news to get around in a hurry."

"Take it, dear, and David will know what to do about it. Oh, I never was so happy," said Miss Jenny.

"Nor was I," echoed Miss Kitty. "Oh, my dear boy, the cloud over you is now all removed."

In a shorter time than would have seemed possible anywhere else, the news spread over the town. The squire, replete with information, admitted he had always had doubts about the drowning and no one in the excitement of the moment reminded him of his earlier words. David Means showed the letter to a chosen few who would see that the truth was broadcast accurately; even Mr. Newcombe shook Robin's hand now in a half shamed accord; the young people flew from house to house and before anyone realized it the wedding list had swelled to enormous proportions; while Alice clung to Robin and in their jubilance there were tears in their eyes.

As to the preparations for what would now be a real "reception," Miss Jenny and Miss Kitty in what might be called a frenzy of happiness called in the caterer and Pearl was completely won over by the increased number of guests to accept his professional assistance.

"Now don't you worry, ladies," Mr. Yates assured the Miss Adairs. "You just leave everything to me an' Pearl here an' we'll take care of all the details. I haven't catered forty years not to know my business. You'll see. Without lifting a finger you'll have the finest collation ever served in this town."

So Miss Jenny and Miss Kitty rested in the pleasure of the great anticipation, saying many prayers for Molly along with their general thanksgiving.

The wedding day was perfect. Not a cloud dimmed the skies. The heat of the week before had subsided into a comfortable warmth. The hours represented late summer at its rich and fragrant best. The whole town seemed to waken early, for this wedding with all its tensions and later relief was like no other. No one ever knew just how the oral invitations were given, but it was well, for the church, decked with its white stocks and gladioli was practically filled when as it neared four o'clock the carriage with Miss Jenny, Miss Kitty and Robin drove up to the door. Those inside went their different ways after tearful kisses from the old ladies as they saw the shining light in Robin's eyes.

Everyone said afterwards that it had been the loveliest wedding the town had seen. The groom so handsome, turning a little from his appointed place at the front to watch his bride as, in breathtaking beauty, she moved slowly up the aisle in her dress and veil like white mist, leaning on her father's arm.

All the sadness that had gone before was lost and forgotten in the hushed, ecstatic moment when Robin and Alice were made husband and wife.

The reception in the stone house, itself a bower of flowers, was one great burst of joy. Mr. Yates, the caterer, as good as his word, had enlisted Pearl to join his regular minions, and even Hepsy, who could not hold out when the day itself came, appeared at the back door and pitched in with the rest. For there was need of help. More and more unexpected guests kept coming.

"And spare nothing, Mr. Yates," Miss Jenny had urged.

He was only too pleased to accept the unusual challenge presented and follow Miss Jenny's instructions.

Such laughter and exclaiming and music and good wishes as flowed through the rooms that afternoon, as the sun began to slant with golden floods over the lawn and the great portico! Surges of happiness seemed to rise from the guests, among whom the old cousins, David Means, the Newcombes and even the squire in his new black suit moved in vain attempts to keep pace with the bride and groom who were drawn here and there on every side.

At last it was time for the leave-taking. Betsy went upstairs with Alice to help her into her going-away dress.

When she came downstairs at last in a pink suit and a hat covered with roses, Robin was waiting at the foot of the stairs, having already made his private good-byes. The big hall was massed with guests, all watching too. When she was almost down Robin reached up, caught her in his arms and kissed her as though they were alone upon the earth! Then he guided her swiftly through the French doors and across the portico. From all sides there came shouts and cries and handfuls of rice and rose leaves. But the young men seemed strangely absent.

Just as Robin and Alice reached the carriage in the drive,

Tom's strong tenor rose, joined instantly by a chorus of male voices. It was their final serenade with the song that had run like a prescient thread through all the courtship. It fell now sweetly on the early evening air.

> O whistle and I'll come to you, my love,
> Whistle and I'll come to you.
> Though father and mother and all should go mad —
> Whistle and I'll come to you, my lad!
> Oh, my love, I'll come to you.